JUNGLE DOCTOR

Spots a Leopard

③

JUNGLE DOCTOR
Spots a Leopard

Paul White

CF4·K

10 9 8 7 6 5 4 3 2

Jungle Doctor Spots a Leopard, ISBN 978-1-84550-301-7
© Copyright 1987 Paul White
First published 1963, reprinted 1965, 1967
Paperback edition 1972, revised edition 1987
Reprinted 1990, 1995
by Paul White Productions,
4/1-5 Busaco Road, Marsfield, NSW 2122, Australia

This edition published in 2007 and reprinted in 2008
by Christian Focus Publications, Geanies House, Fearn, Tain,
Ross-shire, IV20 1TW, Scotland, U.K.
Fact files: © Copyright Christian Focus Publications

Cover design: Daniel van Straaten
Cover illustration: Craig Howarth
Interior illustrations: Graham Wade
Printed and bound in Denmark by Norhaven A/S

Since the Jungle Doctor books were first published there have been a number of Jungle Doctors working in Mvumi Hospital, Tanzania, East Africa - some Australian, some British, a West Indian and a number of East African Jungle Doctors to name but a few.

African words are used throughout the book, but explained at least once within the text. A glossary of the more important words is included at the front of the book along with a key character index.

CONTENTS

Fact File: Paul White

Born in 1910 in Bowral, New South Wales, Australia, Paul had Africa in his blood for as long as he could remember. His father captured his imagination with stories of his experiences in the Boer War which left an indelible impression. His father died of meningitis in army camp in 1915, and he was left an only child without his father at five years of age. He inherited his father's storytelling gift along with a mischievous sense of humour.

He committed his life to Christ as a sixteen-year-old school-boy and studied medicine as the next step towards missionary work in Africa. Paul and his wife, Mary, left Sydney, with their small son, David, for Tanganyika in 1938. He always thought of this as his life's work but Mary's severe illness forced their early return to Sydney in 1941. Their daughter, Rosemary, was born while they were overseas.

Within weeks of landing in Sydney, Paul was invited to begin a weekly radio broadcast which spread throughout Australia as the Jungle Doctor Broadcasts - the last of these was aired in 1985. The weekly scripts for these programmes became the raw material for the Jungle Doctor hospital stories - a series of twenty books.

Paul always said he preferred life to be a 'mixed grill' and so it was: writing, working as a Rheumatologist, public speaking, involvement with many Christian organisations, adapting the fable stories into multiple forms (comic books, audio cassettes, filmstrips), radio and television, and sharing his love of birds with others by producing bird song cassettes - and much more…

The books in part or whole have been translated into 107 languages.

Paul saw that although his plan to work in Africa for life was turned on its head, in God's better planning he was able to reach more people by coming home than by staying. It was a great joy to meet people over the years who told him they were on their way overseas to work in mission because of the books.

Paul's wife, Mary, died after a long illness in 1970. He married Ruth and they had the joy of working together on many new projects. He died in 1992 but the stories and fables continue to attract an enthusiastic readership of all ages.

Fact file: Tanzania

The Jungle Doctor books are based on Paul White's missionary experiences in Tanzania. Today many countries in Africa have gained their independence. This has resulted in a series of name changes. Tanganyika is one such country that has now changed its name to Tanzania.

The name Tanganyika is no longer used formally for the territory. Instead the name Tanganyika is used almost exclusively to mean "the lake."

During World War I, what was then Tanganyika came under British military rule. On December 9, 1961 it became independent. In 1964, it joined with the islands of Zanzibar to form the United Republic of Tanganyika and Zanzibar, changed later in the year to the United Republic of Tanzania.

It is not only its name that has changed, this area of Africa has gone through many changes since the Jungle Doctor books were first written. Africa itself has changed. Many of the same diseases raise their heads, but treatments have advanced. However new diseases come to take their place and the work goes on.

Missions throughout Africa are often now run by African Christians and not solely by foreign nationals. There are still the same problems to overcome however. The message of the gospel thankfully never changes and brings hope to those who listen and obey. *The Jungle Doctor* books are about this work to bring health and wellbeing to Africa as well as the good news of Jesus Christ and salvation.

Fact File: Words

WORDS TO ADD EXPRESSION AND EMPHASIS:
Eheh, Heh, Hongo, Kah, Koh, Kumbe, Ngheeh, Yoh.

TANZANIAN LANGUAGES: Swahili (main language)
Chigogo (one of the 150 tribal languages)

WORDS IN ALPHABETICAL ORDER:

Amekwisha kweda kanisani - he has gone to the church

Bibi - Grandmother

Chewi – leopard

Cibogolo - witchdoctor's box

Dudus – insects or germs

Habari – what news?

Mzuri – old man

Hodi – can I come in?

Ibululu - a fenced-in courtyard.

Ilimba – musical instrument

Kali sana - very fierce!

Karibu - come in

Kifaru - rhino

Kwaheri - goodbye

Mahala matitu - black magic

Mapigi - charms

Mbisi - hyaena

Mbukwa – greetings

Muganga – witchdoctor

N'go - no

Njema – good

Nyau - the cat

Panga - knife

Sana - very much

Shaitan - devil

Sindano - needle

Somaki - fish

Wuchawi - witchcraft

Zimba - buck

Zinzila za sakami - blood vessels

Fact File: Characters

Let's find out about the people in the story before we start. Bwana is the Chief Doctor and the one telling the stories. Daudi is his assistant. Take a moment or two now to familiarise yourself with the names of the people you will meet in this book.

Baruti - hunter

Daudi – Deputee doctor

Dr Suliman – Madole employee

Juma – witchdoctor

Mali - nurse

Mwendwa - the night nurse

Yobwa – Tribesman

Bwana – doctor in charge

Gideon - bus driver

Madole – ex-chief of village

Mboga – hospital worker

Tembo – young sick boy

Yonah - Game Scout.

Fact File: Tuberculosis

Tuberculosis is caused by a bacterial infection. In the 19th century many people in Europe died from TB. As living standards and medicine improved the death toll decreased. However, today three million die annually from this disease. Infection is possible anywhere, but is most common in sub-Saharan Africa and Southeast Asia.

The TB bacteria when inhaled in the form of microscopic droplets are what cause this disease. Coughing, speaking or sneezing causes the small droplets to be expelled into the air. TB bacteria are killed when exposed to ultraviolet light, including sunlight.

The symptoms are chronic or persistent cough; fatigue; lack of appetite; weight loss; fever; night sweats.

An undetected infectious TB victim will, on average, infect another ten cases every year. It is important when it is detected to control the spread of the disease. So all disease carriers must be found, isolated and treated until they are no longer a risk to others. Vaccination is a good way to prevent infection. But if you are travelling in a country where TB is a problem make sure that you eat well and enjoy plenty of sunlight and exercise. Seek medical attention if you develop a cough that persists for more than three weeks.

1
On the Spot

'Where did this leopard attack exactly?' asked the business-like voice of Yonah, the African Game Scout.

'Away over there.' The tall Tanzanian tribesman pointed with his chin and raised his voice to show distance. 'I, Yobwa, heard that it happened there to the south, near the village of Cibogolo.'

Now Cibogolo means 'witchdoctor's box' and was a place where violent things had been happening.

From one of the hair-pin bends of the road cut into the mountainside the two men looked out over the flat sweep of savannah, with its thornbush jungle and huge baobab trees. In a clearing two hundred metres below was a flat-roofed, mud-walled house.

The young man spat. 'That is the house of M'sala. *Koh*! It is a place of death. Since the days of harvest, five who lived there have returned to the ancestors. They...'

The Game Scout interrupted him. 'There have been words of trouble, of black magic?'

'*Kah*! Words?' Yobwa raised his eyebrows. 'Were there words? Great One, you know these affairs of witchcraft, when men of anger speak furtively behind their hands. And *hongo*! Then came this leopard.'

He shrugged.

'Have you actually seen it?'

'No, but one who saw it kill the new leader of this place said it had great spots like the bunched-up fingertips of a man's hand.' He dropped his voice. 'And the right forepaw is like this...' He drew four dots in the shape of a square in the dust then rubbed them out hastily, looking round as though he expected to be spied upon. He moved closer to the Game Scout and muttered, 'The hand of Madole, chief of this village for twenty years, has but four fingers on it.'

'He no longer rules here?'

'Not even a little. In a night he found himself no longer chief, stripped of authority and without power. *Hongo*! And did resentment and jealousy burn in his heart! It is said that he paid the price of many cows to witchdoctors for a medicine of such strength it was possible for him to change himself into a leopard.'

The Game Scout spat. 'Who was given his place?'

Yobwa fingered the charms that were round his neck. 'The eldest son of M'sala had education and wisdom. *Koh*! But before a moon had passed, he was dead, terribly dead. It was the leopard with but four toes that killed him – in the middle of the marketplace at high noon! This is not the way of most leopards.

Many say that there is the cunning mind of a jealous man within that spotted creature's skin.'

The tall tribesman again looked furtively around. Yonah's face was mask-like. He ground out, 'Go on, - what happened?'

'Sickness came like a thunderstorm upon this house but death did not come fast enough to all of them. So again comes leopard.' He shrugged. 'It is a place of fear. All are dead there...' As he spoke, out of the house below them staggered a boy. He stood peering up at them and then fell flat on his face.

The Game Scout jumped behind the wheel of his landrover. They skidded round the curves of the mountain pass, crashed through thornbush scrub and bounced through huge elephant footprints in the black soil. In their path a covey of guinea fowl scuttled away screeching.

The landrover bumped on over what had been a millet garden. There was room for only one wheel on the narrow path.

Unexpectedly and forcibly the driver stamped on his brake. The man beside him shot forward, bumping his chin hard against the windscreen.

'*Yoh*!' he growled, 'why did you do...?' His mouth flopped open. Across the path was a distinct line of white ashes. His voice was tense. 'Let us travel with care.' Both men jumped to the ground and walked at right angles to the path, threading their way through the dead millet stalks. They peered at the ground most carefully before taking a forward step.

At last Yobwa spat in front of him. '*Koh*! The spell of death does not reach as far as this.'

Yonah grunted his assent and hurried across the clearing to where the boy lay.

Striding down the path towards them came a tall, cheerful man with a spear in his hand.

The Game Scout shouted, 'Stop! Look at the path in front of you! Stop!'

The new arrival paused, then deliberately scattered the ashes with his foot. He smiled, '*Habari* – what news?'

'*Njema* – good,' said the Game Scout automatically. Then he stretched out his hand. '*Kumbe*! It is Baruti!' They were both tall, solidly built men.

'*Eheh*, it is I, O Yonah Nhuti, and I have joy to greet you. *Kah*! But is there trouble here?'

'*Eheh*! Great trouble.'

Baruti bent and lifted the boy's head out of the dust. He was painfully thin, and his skin was burning hot.

'Is he dead?' Yobwa stepped back a pace.

'No, but he has much need of strong medicine.'

'*Kah*!' Yonah Nhuti scratched his head. 'I've been sent to deal with this man-killing leopard, and I find myself landed with a sick boy.'

'Let me put him in your machine and give him water to drink,' said Baruti, 'and perhaps we will find a way to help.'

Yonah grunted. He stepped confidently over the place where Baruti had trampled on the witchdoctor's medicine. He threw open the door of the landrover, and put a blanket under the boy's head as Baruti placed him down gently.

'You look after him,' he said gruffly. 'I will seek for the tracks of this great cat.'

Baruti saw that the boy was quite unconscious.

'*Yoh*! He cannot swallow,' he muttered, moistening the boy's feverish lips. 'Truly, he too is very near the ancestors.'

A shout came from the Game Scout, who was down on one knee in the dust near the house. 'Come and look at these tracks! Not only has a leopard been here, but it has walked right round the house, just as if it were a witchdoctor…and look at this!' He pointed to a group of paw marks still clearly seen in the dust.

'*Eheh*!' said Baruti, 'he lacks one finger in his right forepaw.'

Their eyes met. '*Hongo*!' said Baruti. 'You fear this creature?'

'*Koh*!' growled Yonah, 'any wise hunter fears any leopard.'

A cloud of dust was rising into the hot air two kilometres away across the plain. 'Let us drive to the road,' said Baruti. 'This is the bus to Dodoma and it will be the quickest way to carry the boy to the hospital. It will turn a safari of two days into one of two hours.'

At the hospital, we were having a special clinic to try and steal a march on tuberculosis. We had injected a drop of tuberculin into the skin of the forearms of a dozen people. I had just arranged with them when they were to come in again for me to see the result when Mboga, one of the hospital orderlies, came running round the corner.

'Bwana! Baruti, the hunter, has just arrived on the bus...'

'Has he, Mboga? Useful things, buses...'

'*Eheh*, Bwana. They take the weariness out of your feet, and shorten safaris truly...but as I said, Baruti has arrived, with a sick one. He says it is a matter of importance!'

Baruti stood in the shade of a baobab tree with his arm held firmly round a boy who coughed in a way that shook his thin body. The boy groaned and leaned back against Baruti.

'*Mbukwa*!' I greeted.

'*Mbukwa*.' The boy's voice was little more than a husky murmur.

'*Habari*? – what is the news?'

'*Njema* – the news is good, but...' He shook his head slowly. 'Are you the Great One here?'

'I am the doctor.'

'Have you medicines for the Great Cough?'

'Yes, we have many medicines.'

His eyes were bright with fever. He stood unsteadily to his feet. 'I have no gifts to bring for medicines.'

'Have you no relations?'

'In our house,' said the boy, 'were my father, mother, my big brothers, and my small sister. But one who visited us had the Great Cough, and *yoh*...!' He made a gesture with his hands and I realised that tuberculosis, like a bush fire, had swept through their home.

'*Heeh*,' he said, 'what can I do, Bwana? I have no-one. Evil has come upon our house.'

18

A bright yellow landrover came slowly along the road. Mboga, standing directly behind me, whispered very softly, 'That is Juma bin Ali, Bwana. He is a new sort of medicine man and has been causing trouble with the ex-chief, Madole, who has only four fingers. It is said that he is trying to kill the old man with spells.'

Baruti gently sat the boy down with his back to the tree. He moved across to me.

'Bwana, he has small strength, truly. The only strong thing about him is his cough. You must help him.'

'We will, Baruti.'

The boy struggled to stand up, but his knees buckled under him. I picked him up and carried him the rest of the distance to the ward and put him into the hands of Mali, the trained nurse in charge of the men's ward.

'Put him to bed, and keep him quiet. I will come and examine him soon.'

'Yes, doctor.'

Baruti was squatting in the shade of the pepper trees.

'What is his story, O hunter?'

'His name is Tembo and, as he told you, death and trouble have come to his house. It would seem that this Great Cough has struck again and again. Three days ago this boy, his elder brother and his father, all gripped by this sickness, sat in the sun as is the custom of the tribe. They live in a part of the country where there are many animals. Behold, through the thornbush stalked a leopard. He came straight at them. *Pow*! He hit the father and he died. He sprang at the larger boy, who rolled over and over, and this child fainted. When his wisdom returned he was by himself. When I found him he had tasted neither food nor water for two whole days, and *hongo*! If there had been no bus, *kah*! He would have been dead by now.'

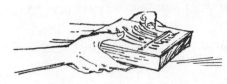

Baruti unslung his *ilimba*, sat down under the pepper trees, and started to play softly.

'*Kah*!' said Daudi as we walked toward the ward. 'He always plays that tune when he has sadness in his heart. And behold, today it seems to well up in him. Have you heard his story? He had four sons and all of them died from tuberculosis when they were young. There is great sadness in Baruti's heart. When he looks at Tembo he sees his own children all over again.'

'From the look of that boy, Daudi, I'd think that we're all facing tragedy. I wouldn't give young Tembo much chance of living even twenty-four hours.'

'*Kah*! Bwana, then he stands at the very gates of death?'

'He does. And our supply of drugs for this disease is desperately small. We need every pill and injection for other sick people. We have hardly any to spare.'

Daudi looked at me quickly. 'You're going to give him a chance?'

'We have to. There's so much more at stake than his body.'

Daudi nodded. 'Shall I test his blood?'

'Yes, please.'

Deftly he took a sample and hurried away to the laboratory. Gently I examined Tembo's chest, and then the whole of his emaciated body. The disease had gone a long way and the further that examination went the further my heart sank.

Baruti stopped his *ilimba*-playing as Daudi came briskly back to the ward with his report. I read, 'Haemoglobin 20%. Malaria parasites present – plus, plus.'

Not only was Tembo suffering from two diseases ranking among the world's worst killers, but his defences were down and his blood was only a fifth of the strength it ought to be.

In English, which Baruti did not understand, I said, 'What Tembo needs first of all is a blood transfusion, Daudi. What about asking Baruti if he'd give a pint?'

Daudi nodded. 'That would be a good thing.'

'Right. Prepare the instruments and the apparatus and I'll see about donors.'

Baruti sank heavily down on a chair and said, 'He will die, Bwana. Many times I've seen it happen before. This is a disease that I hate.' I put my hand on his shoulder.

'Perhaps we can cheat your enemy if we build up the boy's strength a little and give him a better chance to fight the germs of this sickness. It would be like holding a leopard away from its victim with a spear till more help comes, for the medicines we have these days are very powerful.'

Baruti sighed. 'What sort of a spear would you use to hold back this leopard?'

'A bottle of good blood from a healthy man.'

Baruti jumped to his feet. 'Would my blood do?'

'If you are willing to give it and it's the right sort.'

He bunched up his fist and stretched out his arm till the veins stood out. '*Koh*! Test it quickly! Remember, leopards will not wait.'

Daudi appeared through the doorway with a tray of test tubes, needles and syringes. He grinned, 'Leave this to me, Bwana. Come on, Baruti.'

The boy coughed and clutched at his throat. I bent down. 'We understand how it hurts you to cough, to talk and to swallow. If you want to tell us things do so with your fingers. Try and make us understand without talking.'

His eyes told me that he understood. Then they turned towards the window where a bee buzzed as it bumped against the flywire gauze.

'*Eheh*,' I smiled, 'honey, eh? Would you like some? It would help.'

A smile flickered around the corners of his mouth.

'You shall have some straight away.'

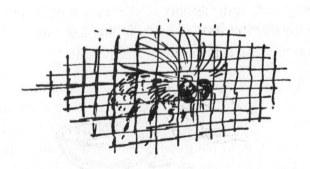

2
Habari – What News?

Mboga came quickly through the door with a small gourd in his hand. He put one finger into it and honey dropped on the floor.

'Carefully!' said Mali, the nurse in charge, hurrying over. She put the gourd near the boy.

'Tembo,' she said, 'go very gently – and don't spill any.'

She came and stood beside me.

'They call him Tembo – the elephant – but he certainly doesn't look like an elephant to me!'

'You're right, it is an interesting name.'

The sick boy was so weak that even dipping his finger into the gourd was a big effort. Baruti, who was looking tired himself, watched the boy's struggles and muttered, '*Kah*! He has so little strength that he cannot lift his head.'

We went outside the door. He put both his hands on my shoulders. 'Bwana Doctor, I have had my blood taken for testing, I have carried that boy in my arms, and brought him on a long safari today – but is it not a thing of hopelessness? What can we do? He is thin and so terribly weak. *Koh*! – there is death written all over him! I have seen this sickness before – many times before.'

'There is some truth in your words. But think. Before you found him this morning he had no chance of life. Now that you have brought him here with speed there is a hope, although it is a slim one.'

'But, Bwana, he can't even swallow!'

'But we can inject.'

'You can't inject food!'

'Can't we, though! Perhaps not porridge and meat and fruit, but we can run fluids into him through a tube and needle…the transfusion first and then many other things to help and strengthen him.'

Baruti stood up straight. I could almost see his mind working. 'These medicines, this food of a special sort that you speak of – will it not cost much money?'

'It will.'

'Who will supply that money?'

'His relations, I hope.'

'But, Bwana, he has none! I am a hunter. I have a

small herd of cattle. I shall bring one of these to pay for the boy's medicines.'

I gripped his hand. 'That is excellent. It will make Tembo feel that someone cares for him. This will help in the struggle. Remember, I too am a hunter and in this battle against these *dudus* of tuberculosis it is a tougher struggle than your friend Yonah Nhuti is fighting against that leopard...'

'*Koh*!' said Baruti, 'I wonder what is happening. He is a man of skill, that Yonah. He shoots in a way that brings death quickly to animals who carry danger in their teeth or claws.'

Daudi hurried up and handed me a report which read, 'Blood of Baruti completely compatible with that of Tembo, the child with tuberculosis, Ward 3, Bed 6.'

'Can I leave this transfusion to you Daudi?'

He nodded. 'We will start at once.'

'Right. Report to me if you have any trouble or, if not, when the last fifty millilitres is being given.'

Daudi looked most professional and said, 'Yes, doctor.'

An hour later a junior nurse called through the window. '*Hodi*, Bwana?'

'*Karibu*.'

'Doctor, the transfusion is running smoothly. There are still fifty millilitres to go. Staff Nurse said to call you now.'

I walked back with her to the hospital and Mali came across to me as I entered the ward.

25

'Doctor, the blood has been collected and is being given in the usual way, and the boy shows no reaction. I have sent Baruti home to bed. He was exhausted and his mind was full of doubts.'

She moved across to Tembo, adjusting the flow of the transfusion. She smiled down at him, took a small spoon, dipped it in the honey gourd, twiddled it round, and held it over his mouth. His lips parted. A drop of honey fell in. He tried to smile. His tongue licked his lips. 'More…?' His eyes answered the question. For a while she sat back.

I watched everything that was happening in a mirror propped up against some books in front of me. In a soft voice Mali said, 'Tembo, there is one person that you must hear about, the most important person in the whole world. His name is Jesus and he loves you, body and soul.'

The boy wanted to speak but it was too much for him.

Mali was on her feet. 'What about a sip of water, and another drop or two of honey.'

He settled his head on the pillow, his mouth opened, his Adam's apple moved up and down and in a hoarse whisper he said, 'Can Jesus do anything for my sickness?'

'Oh yes,' nodded Mali, 'he has those who work for him here. The doctor is one, I am another, and Daudi and the other helpers in the hospital work for him too. Now it is true that not everyone has the Great Cough which does so much harm to your body. But everyone has the great sickness of the soul, everybody has done things which he knows are wrong, and everybody has

26

not done things which he knows to be right. This is the sign of the greatest sickness of all – the sickness of your soul, which Jesus calls sin. Now Jesus is God himself. He is the one who made the world and planned the whole of its doings.'

Hoarsely Tembo's voice came, 'How do you know?'

'The words are here in God's book.' Mali turned up the wick of the hurricane lantern and thumbed over the pages of a well-worn Bible. 'See, it says, "And without him (Jesus) was not anything made that was made."'

'*Hongo*—and does Jesus know about me?'

'Yes, he knows about you and if you speak to him he will listen.'

'But how can he?'

'It is a thing hard to understand but easy to do. We call it prayer. When you speak to him, you ask him to heal the sickness of your soul and he will do it.'

'*Koh*!' said Tembo, 'but I want him to heal the sickness of my body.'

'Sometimes he will do that for you, but always he will heal your soul. You see, he died so that he could do this most important thing of all—this healing the sickness of your soul…'

'*Koh*! But how did he die?'

'Men killed him. They killed him with great pain.'

Fear came into the boy's eyes. 'I do not like pain.'

'Nor did he, Tembo, but he loved you enough to suffer instead of you so that you could have your sin forgiven and the sickness of your soul cured.'

The boy coughed harshly and put his hand to his chest. I stood up. The transfusion was nearly finished. We changed the bottle for a clear solution which contained glucose and salt.

I leant over him. 'Tembo, these medicines that we are giving you will help you. They will stop the pain, and give you strength.'

I filled a syringe and injected two drugs into the rubber tube. We watched them drop into the bottle. Mali looked at me and smiled. She ran her hand over Tembo's pitiably thin arm. '*Kah*! Bwana, I am glad you did that. It would be a thing of cruelty to inject anyone who is as thin as he is if you could find another way.'

Tembo's eyes turned towards the gourd of honey. This time he licked the spoon and then with a little sigh closed his eyes and was asleep.

'Mali,' I whispered, 'he can't have too much rest.'

Next morning I came into the ward. '*Habari*, Mali?'

She shook her head. 'The news is good, doctor, but not very. The food has been running into his veins; the fifth bottle is now in place; but, *kumbe*! he is very ill. His temperature is 105°; his pulse races at 140; and his cough – *yoh-eheh*! It shakes him like a strong wind blowing a thin tree.'

'Keep the medicines going. Keep him quiet.'

'*Hongo*!' she sighed, 'it is a pity that he has to be in this ward. There is so much noise, so much going on. If only we had a ward just for people who are sick like he is…'

'Mali, I agree…but that may yet come.'

'Perhaps if you write a book about it, Bwana…'

'I might do that.'

A long week went by. Again I asked the question, '*Habari*, Mali?'

She sighed. 'The news is good, but not very. To young Tembo, it must have been the worst week of all. Every day he shuts his eyes tight as he sees me come with the syringe and streptomycin.' She turned over the pages of his chart. 'The temperature is lower in the daytime but still the same height at night. *Yoh*! And can he sweat! He cannot speak at all now and it hurts him greatly to swallow. When he can eat and drink without trouble that will be a great step forward.'

Baruti was standing outside the door. I passed on the news to him. He shook his head, '*Koh*! He is no better, and there is so little I can do.'

'When the river comes down in a flood, can you stop it in an hour, or a day? And can you clean up the mess it brings with one broom?'

Around Baruti's neck was his *ilimba*. His fingers found the umbrella-spokes which were its keys. He played a sad little tune and then said, '*Eheh*! It takes time, it takes much work.'

'Look back. A week ago things were very bad. The boy was dying. He could take no food, the disease was burning inside him like a fire... Seven days have passed, yet he still lives. We are giving him food. The medicines are fighting the sickness. This is progress.'

'But I want to do something, Bwana.'

'The biggest thing you can do for him is to pray that God will be with him and keep him quiet and take away his fears.'

'I am doing that, Bwana.'

'Well, keep on. And come in and sit with him and tell him stories of your hunting, and tell him about Jesus. Keep him interested and help to make the days of his great battle for his life go quickly.'

'*Koh*!' said Baruti, 'I want to do something bigger.'

'Those are the biggest things of all.'

Two more weeks went by. Daudi came with a report.

'Doctor, Tembo has been with us a month. His blood has more strength and the malaria parasites have gone, but the tuberculosis germs are many!'

In the ward, I found that Mali was deeply concerned.

'His temperature and pulse are a bit better but Tembo just lies there, Bwana. He does not smile. His eyes stare at the roof. Look into them and you see fear! He is surrounded by it. He is saturated in it.'

'Fear upsets the working of your body and it certainly keeps you from getting better quickly.'

'*Koh*!' said Daudi, 'we may be helping him with his tuberculosis but we are not touching his fear.'

'We have the medicine for it, though, Daudi. In the Bible it tells us that God says, "Do not fear. I am with you. Don't be dismayed, I am your God – I will strengthen you, I will uphold you…" Faith is the antidote to the poison of fear.'

'But how are we to get it into him, Bwana?'

'It is not easy, but remember the Bible tells us, "Faith comes by hearing the message, and the message is the word of God."'

Later in the day Baruti walked up to the hospital with a large smile on his face. In his hand he carried a box.

'Bwana!' he called, 'I have something here which should bring joy to Tembo's heart.'

'What's in your box?'

'Come with me and see what happens.'

We went into the ward.

'May I talk with Tembo?' he asked Mali. She nodded. Baruti went across, bent down and said, 'Tembo, look at this!'

From the box he carefully lifted a hedgehog, but the sick boy took not the slightest notice. I saw the muscles tighten around Baruti's jaw, but his voice did not show his disappointment. He went on.

'Eat one of these, and it tastes like pig – but, *kumbe*! It has many sharp points.'

Still there was no response from Tembo. Baruti's cheerful voice went on.

'Let me tell you the story of the large animal with the large spike on his nose. *Hongo*! This creature brought great fear to my heart and even greater speed to my feet…'

A flicker of interest moved across the boy's face. Baruti's eyes gleamed. He stood at the foot of Tembo's bed, prepared to tell the story with all the appropriate actions.

'There were those who told me that *zimba*, the buck, was in the place near the small lake that is surrounded by tall yellow thorntrees. *Yoh-heh*! And what thorns they are, *kumbe*! And they grow not only on the branches but on the trunk! I walked with care, following the spoor of the buck through the dust, and making sure that the wind blew into my face – the noses of these creatures are full of wisdom. Then I saw four beautiful buck. I crouched down and walked through the tall grass until I could come to a place near enough to throw my spear. You must travel with slowness and with care, for behold, if the birds are disturbed then your hunting is in vain.

'I moved away from the lake – the grass was as high as my middle. I had joy, for this would hide me. I crept on and then it was that my hair stood-up on my scalp and cold sweat stung my eyes, for I heard this noise.' He breathed in and out sharply. 'It sounded like someone using a saw.

'*Kumbe*! Charging towards me, his head down and the great spike on the end of his nose pointed right at me, was Kifaru the rhinoceros! He was coming with speed, and it was three times the length of this ward to the nearest one of those thorntrees. And *yoh-heeh*! Did I run! With nimbleness I jumped and grasped a high branch and swung myself up, up, up that tree!'

'What of the thorns, O hunter?' came a voice from further down the ward.

'*Yoh-heeh*! The only thorn that I thought of in the moments of climbing was the one on the end of the

nose of rhino! And then I came to a limb that was strong, the height of a full-grown giraffe from the ground, and I sat there. And *kumbe*! I was aware suddenly of many thorns…'

'Where were those thorns, Great One?' asked Daudi, grinning broadly.

'*Hongo*!' chuckled Baruti. 'Did I not say I was sitting on the limb?'

Quite unexpectedly Tembo laughed and for the first time in weeks he spoke. 'O Great One – and you were frightened? You – the hunter who has killed a lion with a spear, YOU were frightened?'

'*Eheh*! I was full of fear!'

'*Hongo*! I thought you were a man of courage…'

Baruti grinned widely. 'Courage doesn't mean that you have no fear, Tembo, but you show courage by what you do when you are frightened.' He lifted up the boy's emaciated arm. He bent it at the elbow – the muscles hardly showed at all. Then Baruti bunched up his own biceps. He had a most formidable arm. 'When you have someone strong to protect you, Tembo, someone who loves you and is close to you, this makes fear grow small. Faith in that person is the answer to fear.'

'*Kah*! What is faith?'

'When a strong person tells you that he will protect you if you stand behind him, if you believe he will, you stand there. That is faith.'

Daudi said quickly, 'But, Baruti – you are a man of strength, even though you run from the horn of rhinoceros. Do you have some strong one who protects you, who loves you?'

'Yes,' said Baruti, 'Jesus himself. He says, "Come to me, and I will give you rest." He will give you the peace that keeps your heart and your mind. He is stronger than *shaitan* the devil and he always listens to those of his family who talk to him…'

'And what if you are not in his family?' asked Daudi, seeing that Tembo was about to ask the same question.

'God always hears when anybody asks if they may join his family.'

'Is that in God's book?' asked Tembo.

'Oh yes. It says, "As many as received him, that is, who ask him to come right into their lives, to them he gave the power to become the children of God; to those who believe on his name." I asked him to come into every bit of me,' smiled Baruti, 'and he did – I am one of his family, so I pray to him. Because I am one of his family I can keep close to him and fear goes…'

From far down the ward came a voice, 'Do you not fear the dark things of witchcraft?'

'*N'go*.' Baruti shook his head. 'What happens to darkness when you bring light into it?'

'*Kumbe*! The darkness disappears!'

'True, and therefore you do not fear the dark things

when Jesus, who is the light of the world, comes into your life.'

Mali came walking down the ward.

'Enough talk. Rest now, Tembo. Baruti, go and make music under the pepper trees.'

Daudi came to me a few days later and said, 'Bwana, do you notice the tunes that Baruti plays on his *ilimba* have more joy in them these days?'

'*Eheh*, I have noticed that.' And the reason was soon made clear. Baruti came to the door.

'*Hodi*, Bwana?'

'*Karibu*, come in.'

He came in, sat on a three-legged stool, and scratched his head. 'Bwana, it is a strange thing. The boy was very sick a couple of days ago, and now his eyes seem alive, and he himself – *yoh*! He is improving!'

'Baruti, I would say that for the first time he has turned to travel along the road which can lead to health. He is a boy of good wisdom. I only wish he had more strength in his body.'

'*Eheh*, Bwana – but have you seen his eyes? Until three days ago they looked like those of a dead fish.'

I hit Baruti on the shoulder, hard.

'*Heeh*!' he said. 'Why did you do that?'

'You have said something important – fish! Baruti, this is a way for you to help the boy. It is difficult for

35

him to swallow many sorts of food but fish he could eat. You're one of cunning in hunting animals, do you know the ways of fishing?'

'*Eheh*, Bwana, I know them well.'

'I hear that in the dam on the other side of the hills there are many fish.'

'That is so,' said Baruti. 'There are fish – flat ones, with whiskers. *Heeh*! They look like *nyau*, the cat.' He stood up. 'I am on my way.'

'Before you go, realise that a great change has come to the boy – his fear is less, and for the first time for many days he feels secure.'

3
The News is Good

Baruti covered the twenty kilometres through the thornbush jungle in three hours. He dug for worms and found them speedily. A smile came over his face.

'*Yoh-heeh*! Surely this is a thing of happiness! They are not always easy to find and without bait you fish in vain.'

His line was a coarse one that he had made from baobab fibre. The hook was also of his own manufacture. He threw the line and sat waiting.

Baruti was one of those people who, when he had the opportunity, automatically talked to God. He started off by saying, 'Thank you for the improvement in Tembo's health,' and then he asked God to help him in his fishing. A thought came through his mind – 'Should you ask God to help you to catch fish?' And the answer came back that he was catching them not for his own amusement, nor for his own food, but for a special purpose, which was in line with the plan that he was carrying out for God – the helping of Tembo, the whole of Tembo.

Suddenly the line jerked. It sent a thrill right through his body. He twitched it hard. The pull became stronger still.

'*Yoh-heeh*!' grinned Baruti, 'Bwana fish, the bait is inside your mouth and the hook is now firmly in you!'

It took him five minutes to land a large and aggressive-looking fish. '*Kumbe*!' he smiled as he carefully removed the hook and tied a loop of string round his catch's tail, 'This is a thing of joy. I will try again.'

No new bite came for quite a time and Baruti thought, 'In the Bible, Jesus said to those who went his way that he would make them fishers of men if they followed him.' He looked at his line and said, '*Huh-hmm*, you catch them one by one. Perhaps it takes time. You must come to the right place, you must use the right bait and the right tackle...' And then he thought of Tembo. His fingers still held the line expectantly but he prayed. 'Lord God, please help me to help Tembo to know you as the one who cures his soul and then help me to show him how to put muscles around his soul...'

There was a sudden sharp tug on his line and he landed another fish, about half the size of the first.

He lit a small fire and let the wood burn down to red ashes. He wrapped the smaller fish in bark from a buyu tree, saturated it with water, placed it deep in the ashes, covered it and went back to his fishing.

A voice from behind him greeted, '*Habari*.'

Baruti looked over his shoulder. '*Habari mzuri*. The news of my fishing is good. What is the news of your stomach?'

Baruti's questioner smiled all over his wrinkled face. 'The news is good but the walls of my stomach clasp each other in sorrow.'

'*Koh!*' chuckled Baruti. 'A famine truly is a thing of small satisfaction. Even at this moment there is sufficient meat cooking for both you and me.'

Baruti's line suddenly was alive. He stood to his feet and drew it in. He had to play this one carefully. But just as his catch was half out of the water the line snapped, and the fish went back.

'*Yoh-heeh*! That was a fish of size,' grunted Baruti's companion. 'A thing of sadness to lose it. Many a meal slipped back into the water then.'

'*Eheh*,' said Baruti, 'and I have but one more hook.' He carefully tied it on, baited it and threw the line.

'What's your name, Bwana?'

'Nghani,' replied the old man. 'I am called this because I know all the news of the countryside.'

'Let me tell you some news,' smiled Baruti. 'The fish that I catch will bring strength to a child who would have died if he had followed the old ways. Truly, the hospitals of these days are places of wisdom. This child had the Great Cough. He...'

Nghani interrupted him, tapping him briskly on the shoulder with a bony finger, '*Ohoo*! Your words are not news to me! I know much about this. It is a matter of danger and has more points to it than has a porcupine!'

Then he turned and looked at Baruti keenly. 'Are you not Baruti, the one who makes music and who hunts the animals of the jungle?'

Baruti nodded.

'*Heeh*! I have heard of your strength and skill and how once you killed a lion with a spear.'

Again Baruti nodded.

'Have you ever killed a leopard?'

Baruti shook his head.

'*Heeh*! Indeed, it is a different matter. Leopards are *kali sana* - very fierce! There is a great fuss these days about one particular leopard. It comes from w-a-a-a-y down there.' He lifted the pitch of his voice and pointed due south. 'First it was near the town of Cibogolo but now I hear it is moving up this way.' Nghani dropped his voice. 'It is said that Madole, the chief who is no longer a chief, has the power to turn himself into a leopard...'

Baruti moved his head but said nothing.

'It is said these days that he has with him one who protects him from hostile medicine. He is rich, this Madole. *Kumbe*! He will need all his shillings.'

Nghani stopped for breath. Baruti rolled his eyes as Nghani started again. 'Ever since the new council of the tribe – young men and women mostly – came suddenly with the strength of government and took his power from him in a day, Madole has boiled with rage and done things which smell of deep darkness. But mark my words, Baruti, he will have great trouble! The rumour is that Juma has made medicine that will break his leg…!'

'*Koh*!' said Baruti, 'your tongue produces noises like the rumblings of a hungry elephant's stomach!'

There was a tug on his line. This time he pulled up a good sized fish. He tied it also by the tail to the limb of a thornbush. A large crow with beady eyes flew down and stood looking at the fish. Baruti took no notice. He went across to where his fire was, raked off the ashes, unwrapped the bark, and he and Nghani set to work eating industriously.

Anxious to waste no time Baruti threw in his line again, looping it around his toe.

Nghani suddenly jumped to his feet, made awful choking noises and clawed at the back of his tongue. Then he cleared his throat raspingly and spat.

'*Koh*!' he said, shaking his head solemnly and massaging his throat. 'Surely *somaki* is a food of sweetness to the mouth and consolation to the stomach. *Koh*! But it would be a thing of joy if fish had no bones.'

Baruti smiled. '*Heeh*! That has been said before.'

At that second that almost forgotten fishing line pulled so hard that Baruti nearly lost his big toe. '*Yoh*!' he gasped. 'It is as though I had hooked a hippo!'

Nghani picked up Baruti's spear. The fish fought

41

hard. When it was near the bank, Nghani stabbed with accuracy and they landed another fine fish. As Baruti looped string round the tail of his catch and swung them over his shoulder, Nghani picked up his knobbed stick and said, 'Do not forget my words. Madole has no love for this child whom you help. He has already removed his elder brother. Therefore above all things, look out for leopards.'

Baruti thought of all these things as he strode over the East African countryside. He stopped from time to time to look at rhino tracks, and once there was evidence that elephant had passed that way not long before. The sun was setting as he climbed the last hill and saw the hospital away ahead of him.

That evening, an excited Tembo sat up in bed and ate fish. '*Yoh!*' he said, whispering because he had been warned about his inflamed throat. 'This is truly food. My mouth has joy in it.'

'*Eheh!*' said Baruti. 'And before long your muscles will grow and strength will come back to you.'

At the door, I said to him, 'Well, Baruti, was it worth walking forty kilometres to see that?'

'*Eheh!*, Bwana, but during my walk I have heard words which bring warning of trouble ahead of us. That leopard comes closer and closer.'

4
Sweet Spot

I ran my finger over Tembo's ribs. '*Hongo*! Small Elephant, to do that is like running your hand over a sheet of *bati* – corrugated iron.'

'*Eheh*!' said the boy. 'Bwana, if you had lived for a moon and a half on food run into you through a needle and sips of water, little blobs of honey, thin soup and gruel, you too would have ribs that stick out!'

'Does the fish Baruti caught for you help?'

'*Sana*, very much, and it is easy to swallow for now my throat is not so sore.'

'This is a thing of joy. But above all swallow these pills and eat, eat, eat, that you may grow strong.'

He put his feet out of the end of the bed and grinned at me. 'Bwana, in bed my bones stick right through. Can't I get up even for a little while?'

'Not yet, Tembo, not for some time yet. But we will carry your bed outside into the shade and I have a thing of wonder to show you that will make the days move past with speed.'

Baruti helped me carry the bed through the door. I pointed towards a baobab tree about a hundred metres away.

'Tembo, if I told you that I have a way to make the limbs of that buyu tree seem close as my hand is to you now, would you believe me?'

He looked at me solemnly. 'I don't know, Bwana. It is a thing past understanding. But behold, you would not deceive me. Yes, I would believe you.'

'Look, and you'll know it is the truth!' I produced a small collapsible telescope. 'I am telling you that if you look through this, things that seem far away with your ordinary eye come very close. Now if you believe what I say, then it would be faith if you put it to your eye and looked.'

Tembo amused himself considerably by looking at all sorts of things. In the evening he told Baruti, 'I have been having faith all day.'

'*Yoh*!' Baruti rolled his eyes. 'What do you mean?'

Tembo beamed. 'The Bwana has a machine of wisdom here and when I look through it things that are far away look to be close, and things that I couldn't see with my ordinary eye I can see clearly. The Bwana says that faith is like that. Faith helps us to understand if we use it.'

Mboga came up at that moment. '*Hongo*!' He lifted one eyebrow higher than the other. 'Baruti may be skilful in hunting leopards and lions and fish but there is one thing that I can do that he cannot. I can hunt *dudus* with deep cunning!'

'You shall show us tomorrow,' I laughed. 'Today the shadows grow long and Tembo goes back into the ward.'

Next morning the sun was well up when we carried Tembo, bed and all, to a spot where he could watch Mboga digging fish bones into his tomato garden.

Baruti looked across at him and laughed, '*Mbukwa* – good day, fly catcher!'

'*Hee-heh*!' chuckled Daudi, 'who wants to eat flies? Are you a chameleon?'

Mboga tilted up his nose. 'Great ones, there are no bones in honey. *Kumbe*! Our supplies are running low and Tembo needs honey for his strength and to soothe his throat. Watch now a honey hunter of cunning…'

He went across and asked Mwendwa, the senior nurse on duty, for a little of the powder that was used for irritable stomachs. He went outside. There was a hibiscus bush against the wall with several bees burrowing deep into the red flowers. Standing on tiptoes, with infinite care, Mboga spread a little of the fine white powder over their wings and bodies. The bees backed out of the flower and flew heavily away. Mboga hurried after them.

'*Yoh-heh*!' he cried. 'They cannot fly as fast as usual – and I can see them because of the white powder!'

Tembo turned over on his stomach bracing the

small telescope against the end of his bed and followed every move.

'Watch him carefully. Tell us exactly what happens.'

The boy's excited voice came huskily, '*Kumbe*! He runs with strength. He stops and looks about. He walks on slowly. He runs again. He looks up. He jumps to the north, and see - *yoh*! – he climbs.'

Mboga was swarming up a buyu tree about half a kilometre from the hospital. He swung himself higher and higher.

'*Kumbe*!' grunted Daudi, 'here comes trouble! While Mboga is experienced in the matter of honey his knowledge is not wide when it comes to bees! *Hongo*! Let's go down there, Bwana.'

I put a restraining hand on the sick boy's shoulder. 'Keep watching, Tembo, and don't use your voice unless you have to.'

He nodded but his eyes were glued to the telescope. 'Bwana – he has put his hand into a hole in the tree – he's pulling out honeycomb – he's starting to eat it!'

'*Kumbe*!' said Daudi. 'Quick, Bwana, run!'

I saw him grab a box of matches and we dashed down towards the tree. Daudi stopped several times to pick up some brushwood. He panted, 'The bees will have no joy in losing their honey...but smoke may keep them quiet and perhaps...'

But before the fire was smoking properly the bees registered their disapproval in their traditional way. Mboga was cramming honeycomb into a tin. Suddenly he let out a piercing yell, fumbled with the tin, and dropped it.

Bees swarmed angrily around him. He twisted sideways, grabbed at a limb and hung there. An agonised expression spread over his face as his toes groped for a toehold. The honey on his fingers made the bark slippery and one by one they lost their grip. Mboga yelled, slipped and in a second was wedged sideways between the trunk and a limb.

Daudi was desperately throwing green leaves on his small fire and smoke was rising in clouds.

There was only one way to free Mboga – we needed a ladder. I ran back to the hospital. Tembo was laughing so much he could barely speak.

'Bwana – *heeh*! – he's caught in the tree! He can't get up, he can't get down, he beats with vigour at the bees with his hands to the north, and with his feet to the south, but still they attack him. *Yoh*! How he is bitten – and the fire beneath him – the smoke goes up and keeps some of the bees off, but not all, and he yells, his mouth works – *heeh*! How it works...!'

In the distance came yells from the baobab tree and roars of laughter from every direction. I caught up an old mosquito net and a pair of surgical gloves. Baruti grabbed one end of the ladder and we scurried back to the tree. Angry bees zoomed around us. It was hard to avoid being stung.

Mboga could not have been more uncomfortable. In front of him was a great hole in the tree. A voice shouted advice, 'Mboga, why do you not crawl into the trunk of the tree? We hear there are snakes inside and they might not bite as hard as the bees!'

'*Yoh-heeh*!' howled Mboga, 'help me! – I have no joy in this situation!'

I draped the mosquito net over me and struggled up the ladder. The smoke made it hard to see and the mosquito net made it hazardous to climb. But at last I was at the top and able to wedge one foot into the hole of the tree and brace the other against a rough spot on a limb. I gripped Mboga under the armpits and lifted. He didn't budge. I heaved harder. There came a rending tear and a look of horror spread over his face.

'Bwana! I am moving… *heeh*! But my shorts also…'

A bee alighted on a patch of skin that had suddenly come into view in the place where Mboga's hip pocket used to be. I was laughing so much that it was hard to balance. After a final heave Mboga was hanging desperately by his hands while his legs dangled six metres from the ground. His shorts flapped like a flag at half-mast.

'Bwana!' he yelled. 'Knock that bee off! I can't hold on and deal with it as well!'

As I stretched forward to swat the offending insect a burning pain stabbed my arm and another behind my knee. Baruti pushed the ladder into place under Mboga. He scrambled down and the bees turned on me. The mosquito net was all that separated me from their anger. The ladder felt good under my feet and the ground even better.

'The net,' mumbled Mboga through his swollen lips, 'give me that net.' He put it over his head and draped it carefully over his damaged shorts.

Baruti picked up the tin of honey. 'All is not lost,' he chuckled. Mboga looked balefully round at him. He was largely covered by the mosquito net and I found it very hard not to laugh while Daudi whistled the tune of the bridal march as Mboga stumbled up the path.

A quarter-of-an-hour later, Mboga was sitting on a petrol box anointing himself here and there with ointment to stop the swelling and the pain.

'Well, was the honey worth it?' I asked. He looked at me, his eyes twinkling between swollen lids.

'*Eheh*, Bwana – honey soothes famines, you know, and it is good medicine for those whose throats have trouble in them.' Then he chuckled. 'And also, there is no better medicine for anybody than laughter – and, *kumbe*! Everybody in the whole place has had a big dose of that!'

He dabbed industriously for a while and then pointed to a place between his shoulder blades. 'There is still a sting there, Bwana. Please get it out for me.'

5
Four Fingers

Mboga looked at me through half-closed eyes, 'Bwana, have you ever stepped on a snake?'

'*Eheh*!' said Daudi. 'And have you ever put your hand on a scorpion?'

I smiled. 'I have done both those things. Also there was the occasion when I stepped unwarily on a safari of large black ants.'

'*Eheh*,' grinned Mboga, 'then you can understand what lies ahead of us in the hospital here.'

There was the furious honking of a motor horn and a superior looking young African in a light blue suit came stalking down the path.

'Come at once!' he ordered, beckoning me. 'Madole the chief has arrived. He has great trouble. Therefore, come at once!'

'*Yoh-heeh*!' said Mboga. 'Don't go, Bwana. Take no notice of his rudeness.'

Daudi grinned at me. 'He thinks that by speaking as he has he will make himself large and you small.'

'That may be, but I think we had better go up and see the sick one. Our work is to stop pain and to fight death.'

'Truly,' said Daudi quietly, 'but realise that this is a matter of difficulty. He is one of the new way. He is educated and cunning. He seeks the riches of the old man who pays him much for his work and it is greatly to his advantage for Madole to stay alive. *Koh!* We are in trouble.'

A man came running up the path. 'Bwana! Tell Mboga to come down and help us with the pump that brings water to the hospital. It is dead.'

'Can you fix it, Mboga?'

'*Eheh*, Bwana, I will go with him down towards the river.'

'We shall see one another when you've cured it.'

He nodded, grinned and disappeared at the double.

Daudi and I came to a modern station wagon standing in front of the hospital gate. In the back, propped up on pillows, was an old man. I greeted him.

'*Habari*, Mzee? – what's the news?'

'The news is good…' His voice was querulous. 'But I have two great troubles.' He pointed to his leg and winced with agony and then caressed his thin midriff with a trembling hand – a hand that lacked the index finger.

There was a mumble of voices behind me. Then the

54

young man in the blue suit stepped forward.

'I,' he said, 'am Doctor Suliman and I inform you that the Great One demands that he should be given special treatment and care.'

Daudi rolled his eyes and replied, 'If you are a doctor, why do you not give him special treatment yourself?'

'My pain – my pain – my pain!' groaned the ex-Chief.

Doctor Suliman looked at Daudi distastefully and said, 'I am not that sort of doctor.'

I quickly examined the old man and it was obvious that his leg was in a bad way. A stretcher had been brought. 'Carry him at once to the operating theatre,' I ordered.

A blue-suited figure stepped aggressively between the old man and myself. 'Anything that you do must be agreed to by me!'

I kept my voice calm. 'It's necessary first to examine him and see what's to be done. If you care to watch you may do so through the window.'

He shrugged and then spoke in Swahili, 'And what steps are you going to take to accommodate those of us who have come with him?'

Daudi's voice was quiet and controlled. 'This is a hospital, not a hotel. We will happily receive the sick of any tribe, of any religion, be they from Africa, Asia, or Europe, but if the relations desire to stay they must make their own arrangements.'

'This is highly inconvenient!' stormed Doctor Suliman.

'Nevertheless,' said Daudi, 'this is the state of affairs. Come, we will carry the sick one to the place of examination.'

Madole kept up a mumbled background of, 'My pain! My pain! My leg - *ooh!* My leg! *Eeh!* My stomach! *Eeh* - my leg!'

Close behind came Doctor Suliman waving an umbrella and shouting. 'The Chief will refuse any treatment to which I do not agree. He says that at once he must be carried to the place where he will sleep, not to this operating theatre. He says…'

As far as I could hear all that the old man was saying was, 'Oh - my pain! Oh - my leg! Oh - my stomach!' I bent down and said to him, 'Madole, we will ease your pain and then try to find out the cause of it.'

Doctor Suliman grabbed at the shoulder of one of those who was carrying the stretcher. It jerked, jolting Madole's leg. He let out a yell.

I caught Baruti's eye. 'Give this man in blue an opportunity to sit and stay seated.' His eyes twinkled. His arm shot out, gripping the blue sleeve. The enraged young man lifted his umbrella to strike but Baruti twisted and the bogus doctor found himself suddenly sitting rather hard on a handily placed three-legged stool.

We went into the operating theatre and shut the door. I bent over the old ex-Chief. His pulse was rapid and weak. He was shocked and in considerable pain. His right leg was broken above the ankle and it was twice the size of the left. Daudi looked questioningly at me, 'Shall we stop his pain, doctor?'

'Yes, Daudi - a hundred milligrams of pethidine,

please.' He drew the amount up into a syringe. I checked the dose and he injected.

Madole yelled as the needle went in.

'*Yoh*! Madole, that didn't hurt you!'

'*Heeh*!' he quavered, 'I thought it was going to… don't you understand? My trouble is great! Six days now - six whole days, and my eyes have been kept from sleep by pain - pain - pain!' He ground his teeth in a way that was horrid to hear.

'Then why didn't you come in here earlier?'

He looked at me and shrugged. 'That is my affair.'

'Your leg also is your affair. The reason for the swelling and the pain is this delay.'

The old man lifted himself on his elbows. 'Who's delaying now? Get to work!' he screamed, 'and do it now - now!' He sank back exhausted. Gently, Daudi set to work to clean up the injured leg.

Baruti was beckoning to me through the fly-wire outer door of the operating theatre. I went over to him.

'Bwana, much news.' He spoke softly and fast. 'This so-called doctor, Suliman, is a mixture of medicine man and witchdoctor. He knows little of the cunning of the old men who did these things in the tribe and he knows nothing of the work of hospital doctors except the words that they use.' He dropped his voice still lower. 'The reason they delayed bringing Madole in is that Juma bin Ali had made medicine which he said would break the old man's leg. Now this blue-coated one and the evil old man have been up to all sorts of witchcraft and devilry. They went to a man's house to place medicine across his doorway. They had with them four walking sticks, on the bottom of each a leopard's foot was carved, one with only four fingers. But Juma had heard that they were coming and a deep hole was dug along the path that they must follow. *Kumbe*! Down fell the old man and crack went the bones in his leg.' Baruti grinned. 'They dared not call for help from those who could give it in their part of the country. Doctor Suliman! *Heeh*! It would give me joy to spit!'

He looked reflectively round the operating theatre and we both grinned.

'He's in trouble all right. And *hongo*! He comes here to the hospital and who should be setting up practice as a medicine man within sight of us here but the very one who is his bitter enemy!'

'*Heeh*!' said Baruti, 'it is all a tangle of trouble and will lead to much more.'

'Thank you for the news, Baruti.'

I went back to Daudi.

'*Hmmm*,' he said, 'if that blue-suited person is a doctor, he is a peculiar one. See these deep cuts in the skin! Not even a medicine man would do them as crudely as that…' The deep cuts in the skin were all infected.

'Did you go to the hospital at Iringa to see the Medical Assistant there?' I asked.

Madole's face twisted in pain. 'Should I go there? Should I suffer insult? I, who for twenty harvests have been the Chief of my mountain? Should I go there and be merely one among a number of others - and wait?'

He spat viciously and fortunately accurately through the door. The pain-controlling medicine was having its effect. He made no protest as I ran my finger down the side of his swollen leg. It was like touching a balloon.

'The best we can do, Daudi, is to put a supporting plaster cast round this leg. We can't set it properly until he's been to Dodoma for an X-ray.'

Through the window came an angry voice, 'He shall not have it X-rayed! I refuse permission!'

From the path behind him came a sarcastic voice speaking in Swahili, '*Ngheeh*! He whose loud voice you hear is a medicine man of many words and little usefulness! He it is who protects the old one whose life is surrounded with witchcraft. Have you not heard that old Madole has only four fingers? Have you not heard that he can turn himself into a leopard whenever he wishes? Have you not heard that this leopard is coming closer and closer to this village? This leopard kills men therefore the man inside its skin is a murderer!'

I saw the broad shoulders in the blue coat turn from the window and confront a stocky figure in khaki.

'You lie, Juma bin Ali!' He shouted. 'It is your medicines that have brought trouble upon this poor old man who has lost his chieftainship!'

Juma laughed harshly. 'Words!' he gibed, 'words! However, anyone who brings trouble to that old villain would be doing a good thing!'

Suliman's hand flew to his pocket. He whipped out a spring knife and leapt forward. Baruti was still holding Madole's umbrella. He neatly hooked the wrist holding the knife with the crook of the umbrella and pulled. The knife clattered to the ground and Baruti put his foot on it.

Daudi grinned at me. '*Hongo*! Things are happening fast, Bwana. Just as well Baruti was there!'

'Come,' I said, 'let's finish this plaster.'

We moulded it into place. The injection had made our old patient quiet and sleepy. We lifted him onto the stretcher again and carried him out of the theatre door.

Panting, a man rushed up, pushed his way through the crowd and shouted, 'Bwana! Trouble - down by the river - a leopard sprang on a man - they carry him in now! If there are those that fear the sight of blood, let them hide their eyes...!'

The evening quiet was suddenly broken by ragged drumming, beating on tins and blowing of whistles.

'Behold!' said the messenger. 'They already prepare to keep the leopard from their houses! It is a creature of strange ferocity.'

The alarm signal sounded shrill and full of fear. It was taken up in various corners of the village, and the crowd round the hospital melted away.

As we carried the old man across the courtyard Daudi said, '*Koh*! You can feel the tension, Bwana. You can almost smell fear! *Heeh*! Right through the village, doors are shut, windows are barred and hands grip axes and spears.'

Mwendwa was the staff nurse on duty. She clutched a hissing pressure lamp and came towards us.

'Shall I prepare for an emergency in the theatre, doctor?'

'Please, Mwendwa - and make sure that none of your staff goes outside into the dark unless it is unavoidable.'

She nodded.

We carried the old man into the ward. His bed was directly opposite Tembo. The boy was sitting up gaping as he saw Madole brought in. His eyes opened wide with fear. He dragged the sheet over his head and the whole of his bed trembled.

'*Koh*!' muttered Daudi. 'This will do him no good, Bwana.'

Baruti was beside me speaking quietly. 'What shall I do with the knife of the one in blue clothing?'

'Keep it in your pocket, Baruti. I don't want anyone else to start operating this evening!'

His face was grim as he told me, 'Bwana, the man who was attacked by the leopard is Mboga!'

6
Game Scout

I have always had a soft spot for Mboga. He has a nimble sense of humour. On the way to the operating theatre I thought of the many cheerful and kindly things he had done for me and for others.

He was lying on a stretcher in the small room that housed our medical instruments and equipment. Although he looked an appalling mess still there was a twinkle in his eye.

We bent over to hear his husky voice. 'Bwana, it is not all blood. Some of it is oil.'

'A little silence,' said Daudi, 'would help in the matter.'

It looked as though a gang of bandits had set upon poor Mboga. But although his scalp had been lifted right up, his skull was intact. I put a sterile towel over his wounds.

'Tell me in a handful of words what happened.

Then I am going to give you an anaesthetic and repair you.'

His eyes still twinkled. '*Chewi* the leopard sprang on me from behind the roots of the fallen buyu tree by the pump house. I saw a flash of yellow and his burning eyes and great white teeth and then, *wham*! His paw hit me. But even as it hit, I threw the tin of old engine oil I was carrying into his snarling face. *Yohheeh*! It was just as well it was old engine oil - how often have you said we must waste nothing in this hospital!'

Daudi smiled at me and said, 'That is enough, wordy one, the Bwana would work.'

'*Eheh*! But before I work, Mboga, we will ask God's help.'

Quietly I prayed and then Daudi started the anaesthetic. Sometime later, as the last stitch was put in, Daudi looked up expectantly.

'Shall we follow the routine and give a big dose of penicillin to keep ahead of trouble?'

'Please, Daudi. If all goes well, Mboga will have only a row of stitches to remind him of this adventure.' I picked up the pressure lamp and a *panga* - a big jungle knife. We all shared the uncomfortable feeling that lurking in the shadows might be a great spotted beast.

I opened the door. Sitting outside the men's ward in the dark playing his *ilimba*, but with a spear stuck in the ground close to his hand, was Baruti.

We put Mboga into the bed next to Madole, who was keeping up his miserable dirge of, 'My pain - my pain - my stomach - my pain!'

'Madole, you must stop that row! You are disturbing other people!'

'*Koh*! But what of my pain! My leg - yes, you have helped my leg a little, but my stomach - you have done nothing for my stomach!' His voice reached a high-pitched wail. Mali looked at me pleadingly.

'Stop him, Bwana. Everyone else will be in pain unless you do!'

We gave him a white powder to swallow. This didn't satisfy him at all. 'Give me a needle - a needle! *Sindano*! I need a needle!'

Daudi looked at me questioningly. I nodded. 'You shall have it, O Complainer.'

That injection of boiled water worked within five minutes. As the old man became quiet Tembo's scared face appeared above his blanket. I moved close to him.

'All's well, Tembo.'

His lip trembled. 'But, Bwana, that old man over there can turn himself into a leopard - the same leopard that killed my brother, and my father, and the others...' Tears ran down his cheeks. Baruti put his hand on the boy's shoulder.

'Tembo, they say that this ferocious leopard is Madole over there because it has lost one of its fingers. But these cannot be words of truth for was not the Bwana working on his leg at the very time when the leopard attacked Mboga? If a man could turn himself into a leopard, he could not be a man and a leopard at the same time.'

'Also,' said Daudi, 'if Madole could do these magic things would not the leg of the leopard also be broken? Would he only have four toes, like Madole, and not have a broken leg, also like Madole?'

'*Eheh*!' said Mali. 'And would not the leopard's stomach be saying "My pain my pain?"'

Chuckles went through the ward.

'*Kah*!' whispered Tembo, 'I feel safe in this ward because God is here.'

'*Eheh*!' said Baruti, 'that is a good thing. But real safety is more than that. I feel safe because I am one of God's family and God never lets his own children suffer more than they can bear, though he does let them be tested so their faith will grow stronger. Remember that faith is the answer to the poison of fear.'

We walked through the door into the darkness. Baruti paused with a look of serious concern on his face.

'Bwana, we must realise that not one of us is safe while that leopard is about. I do not think God wants us to take risks.'

Through the wire gauze we heard two sick men talking in loud whispers. 'I have thankfulness within me that I do not stand in the same shoes as the Bwana, who must mend the leg of that skin filled with misery!'

The reply came, '*Heeh*! I have thankfulness that it is not I who walks out there in a night full of leopards.'

I pumped up the pressure lamp. Baruti walked over. 'Would you like company on your journey to your house, Bwana?'

'I would indeed.'

* * *

Nothing unusual happened that night and next morning at the hospital Daudi touched me on the shoulder.

'Bwana, come and look at this. It will bring joy to your heart.'

Under the grey-green pepper trees were three people - two boys in beds, and between them sat Baruti, reading to them from a book.

'*Hongo!*' said Daudi, 'he does much of that. I heard him say this morning when Tembo asked him how you could get faith, "Faith comes by hearing and hearing by the word of God." He does much to help, does our Baruti...'

Suddenly Tembo picked up the telescope that I had given him. '*Yoh!*' he cried, 'Great One, look over there!'

'*Heeh!*' said Daudi. 'They drive with speed, those ones.'

We watched a Landrover come rocketing up the hill. It was a wild piece of driving. Round the corner it skidded and ground to a halt. There was a smell of dust and hot oil. From the vehicle staggered a tall man in the uniform of a Game Scout. He took two steps, straightened up for a moment and then collapsed. There was a long, angry gash in his arm.

'Bwana,' said Baruti, 'this is Yonah Nhuti himself!'

Tourniquets, forceps, catgut and stitches came into action.

A quarter of an hour later, he lay back and said thickly, 'Bwana, there is a leopard, a man-killer, near Lolo village. At dawn came the order that I was to shoot it. *Kumbe*! But going down the hill to the village I stopped near the great rocks to look around. My hand was still on the hand brake when...' He leant over, took hold of a cup and drank deeply. He put it down with a shaking hand. 'Bwana, that leopard came at me and sprang right through the windscreen of the Landrover! A piece of glass sharp as a knife gashed me and I bled.'

'What about the leopard?'

'He didn't understand glass. The crash made him wary for his face too was cut. He leapt off and I drove here with speed. *Yoh*! And how my head goes round and round...'

'*Eheh*!' said Baruti. 'It is not the habit of leopards to kill men rather than monkeys. There must be a twist in this creature's mind, Yonah.'

The Game Scout agreed. 'But men will die before that spotted cat does. He has much of the devil in him.'

Sunset came. The place was quiet. There was little wind to stir the hot tropical air which was heavy with the scent of frangipani. In the ward Yonah Nhuti lay shivering. His injury had brought on malaria. Baruti was sitting beside him.

'Leopards are dangerous brutes.'

Yonah nodded. 'The fiercest!'

'This one, you fear, will do much damage?'

'That is indeed my fear.'

'Then what should we do?'

The Game Scout shrugged his massive shoulders and his face twitched with pain as the stitches bit into his skin. 'It will be seven days before I can do anything - this arm cannot handle a rifle.'

Baruti nodded. 'My fear is for this week ahead, for today even!'

'*Eheh*!' agreed the injured man, 'this time of sunset and dusk is when leopards walk. Their eyes see much when the eyes of men see little.'

Mboga had been sitting up quietly in bed. Through the mass of bandages which covered his head came his voice. 'Those are words of truth. Last night when that great spotted cat sprang onto me it was as though death had blown in my face.'

Baruti asked, 'Did you have fear?'

'*Eheh*! I had fear.'

Tembo's mouth was open. He sat tense, too frightened to listen and yet too interested to miss a word.

'What were you frightened of, Mboga?' I asked.

'Teeth and claws and pain, and I suppose death, Bwana.'

'*Kah*!' said Baruti, standing up. 'Death has no teeth for me.'

Mboga shuddered. 'I'll never forget those glittering

eyes and that snarling mouth! They spoke to me of death - loudly!'

Baruti broke in quickly. 'The thing that puts fear into death is when your back is turned to God and your face and your thinking is in the opposite direction to the only one who can help.'

Daudi nodded. 'Your words are true. The Lord Jesus is the only one who matters when death blows in your face or, for that matter, when you walk the ordinary ways of life.'

From behind came Tembo's voice softly. '*Koh*! I would not dare to look into God's face.'

'Why?' said Daudi.

'Because there are things I have done which give me shame.'

'It is Jesus who forgives you for these things,' said Daudi. 'He always forgives anyone who asks Him.'

Madole was lying asleep with his mouth open. Suddenly he yelled and everybody jumped. Then he grunted and sank back into deep sleep.

'*Hongo* everyone!' I picked up my lantern. 'Follow the ways of sleep. *Kwaheri* - goodbye.'

Baruti came outside with me. '*Kwaheri*, Bwana. If you have to come to the hospital in the darkness, carry a lantern, also a big *panga* knife. If you meet a leopard, go for his eyes.'

Lying in bed I listened to the drums being beaten for miles around. It was a ragged jumble of sound aimed at keeping the leopard away. There was a thread of fear woven into that throb of the drums.

7

Walking Bones

Mwendwa, the night nurse, gave me her report. 'At dawn Madole started,' she sighed. 'First it was groans and grunts but now he is shouting and yelling. Tembo is sick again. His cough is worse, his temperature is going up and so is his pulse. He lies there with his head under the bedclothes. He is very upset.'

'What about Yonah Nhuti?'

She smiled wearily. 'He is a bit better, Bwana. The malaria has gone but his arm is stiff and sore.'

'*Mmm*. The first step is to set the old man's broken leg. That will stop a lot of our troubles.'

Mwendwa sighed. 'Don't forget leopards and that damage-doer Juma.'

Across the ward came Madole's querulous voice, 'My pain - my leg - my stomach!' He lay in bed, his mouth sagging open, pulling at the bedclothes. His hands couldn't keep still. I tried to listen to his chest.

He screamed, 'Take that thing away!' and tore at my stethoscope. Carefully I put his hands by his sides.

'Gently, Great One! This is merely a way of listening to the sound of your breathing and to check the way your heart is working.'

He was quiet for a little while and as I listened to his heart sounds I realised that all was not well. I picked up his left arm. 'It will help if we examine the strength of the *zinzila za sakami* - the blood vessels.'

He looked at me suspiciously.

'There will be no pain, only tightness about your arm.' But as I pumped up the blood pressure machine, he suddenly let out a string of curses, threw up his arms and struck wildly at me. I clutched the apparatus in the nick of time or it would have been smashed.

His wild efforts dramatically upset his heart. His eyes dilated, his lips went blue and he clutched at his chest. 'I am dying!' he gulped.

'One of the small heart pills, Mwendwa, quickly!' She brought me a bottle. I tried to slip a pill between his lips. He closed his teeth like a trap.

'This will help you, Madole. Open your mouth, smartly, now!'

He hissed through his teeth and locked them even tighter. Then his eyes rolled, he started to claw at his throat, his mouth fell open and I slipped the pill under his tongue. Its effect was almost magical. In less than a minute, he was himself again.

'Any more of those attacks and he is to be given a pill at once, Mwendwa. Keep the bottle handy on the ward table here. Leave it there all the time.'

I wrote the treatment on the medical chart that hung above his bed and saw for the first time the disapproving face of Suliman.

I turned to Madole. 'We will take you today to Dodoma so that your leg may be set. It is not possible to place the broken ends of bone in line unless they are watched under an X-ray screen.'

Suliman shrugged and turned his back on me. 'He will refuse to have anaesthetic!'

Daudi had come into the ward. 'Turn and speak face to face with the doctor,' he snapped.

Suliman swung round, his eyes blazing and shouted, 'We refuse - no anaesthetics! No X-rays!'

I tried to keep calm. 'If we don't give him anaesthetic we can't set the leg. If we can't see the bones in an X-ray we can't set the leg. If we don't set it he will die.'

Suliman stood staring. Then he strode over to the old man's bed and spoke rapidly in language I didn't understand.

'I will fix this matter if you wish, Bwana,' said Daudi. An hour later he wiped his forehead as he reported, '*Hongo*! It was a debate of many words. At last they agreed, but they demand to go to Dodoma in their station-wagon.'

'Tembo will be happy about that. We'll take him in and have his chest X-rayed but I doubt that it would be wise to take him in the same vehicle as Madole. It's amazing what harm that old man's presence has done to him. He's lost a month's progress in a week.'

An hour later Tembo, lying on a mattress and propped up on pillows, was in the back of the Landrover. His eyes kept turning towards the station-wagon which followed in our dust.

We drove down the long hill from the hospital. There was no little interest in our safari.

Juma, the modern-style medicine man, carefully focused a powerful pair of field glasses and watched us out of sight. There was an ugly smile round his thick lips. He walked across to his Landrover and deliberately pumped up the tyres.

Nearly a kilometre away Baruti was watching both cars disappear into the heat haze, when towards him limped Yonah Nhuti, his arm in a sling.

'*Habari*?' he greeted.

'*Njema* - the news is good,' replied Baruti, 'but as you will have seen, our enemy walks where he wills.'

Yonah nodded. 'I saw the spoor in the dust near the hospital gate and also in the moist sand of the river bed, and the paw marks were clear cut. It was old Four Toes all right. He has strength, that one!'

'*Eheh*,' agreed Baruti, 'and also cunning. See - from here his tracks cease. He travels only on rock.'

They walked together to the crest of a small hill. They could see for a considerable distance in any direction. Below them stretched the winding dry river bed with its occasional moist patches. Beyond it, the green of the maize gardens and the still darker green places where peanuts were planted. Between them and beyond, winding through the huge baobab trees, was the red ribbon of road.

'Look at that,' said Baruti. 'The dust of the Bwana and those that are with him has scarcely settled, and see who comes!'

On to the road moved Juma's bright yellow Landrover. Yonah spat. 'It is my work to shoot leopards, but *hongo*! Within me is a voice which says that Juma is more dangerous than any leopard, and that includes Four Toes!'

'I agree,' said Baruti, 'but come, let us trace this animal of danger. Perhaps we will find something to guide us.'

They started to walk slowly in a wide circle. An hour later they met. Both shook their head and Baruti said, 'The ground shows nothing, but over there the sky has its paw marks also…'

Their eyes focused on a dozen slowly circling vultures.

The thirty kilometre drive to Dodoma was an ordeal for Tembo. Mboga tried to make time pass more quickly by telling stories. 'Over there,' he said, pointing to a large thorn bush, 'from behind that very tree came Kifaru the rhino one day. He chased us down this hill with great speed. *Hongo*! My blood turned to water - *kumbe*! - and the Bwana let him come so close that his breathing cut into me like a saw and his nose was almost into the back when the Bwana put his foot on the small pedal and we climbed with speed.'

Tembo's hand clutched the seat beside him and a fit of coughing shook him. Mboga looked at me questioningly and I nodded. He went on...

'See over there, the large grey rocks? *Ooh-heeh!* Is that alive with baboons! See, on the top sits an old one, watching, ready to warn. *Kumbe*! He would not be looking like that if there were any leopards in this part of the country.'

Fear twisted the boy's face. There was silence but for his coughing and the bumping of the Landrover over the rough road. At long last Mboga said, 'See? Over there - a huge rock, shaped like a crouching lion? Beneath that is Dodoma...'

For the first time Tembo spoke. 'Bwana, what are they going to do to me? What will happen?' He was shivering.

'There is a machine of wisdom called X-ray, Tembo. You stand with your back to it. In the room where the work is done they turn on a switch and light goes through your body and we can see how your lungs look. It hurts not at all and by this we are able to know the best way to make you strong again.'

Tembo looked from Daudi to Mboga. 'This is true,' said Daudi. 'And remember that Madole also will have his leg placed so that we may see the bones inside it and how to mend them. He has greater fear than you have and if you stand there with courage this will be a great thing.'

'You will be there, Bwana, and Daudi?'

'Yes, we will be there.'

'And Bwana, must I stay there while they work on… on…the old man?'

Mboga looked at me. 'If the Bwana says so, you and I could go outside while work is done on Madole.'

'This would be a good thing, Tembo. There is a little room where you can sit with Mboga till we have finished.'

Ahead was a signpost: Zambia 600 km south, Lake Tanganyika 450 km west, Kenya 500 km north.

We crossed the railway line and drove down to the hospital.

The African Medical Officer was a most competent doctor. He shook my hand and said, 'Bring your patients into the X-ray room. What are their troubles?'

'A boy whose chest I want to screen and an old man with a broken leg that I would like to set under anaesthetic. Could we screen the boy first?'

He nodded. Daudi bent down and spoke to Madole, '*Kah*! Great One, rest from your teeth-grinding. The Bwana has arranged for the boy to be examined first so that you may see that this is a way of wisdom and not of pain. Watch what is done with a mind that understands and then make your choice, but make it with wide open eyes. Say no to this sleep medicine and you close the only path to the recovery of your leg. Say no and you will say "finish" to your life.'

There was a hiss as the electric current was turned on. The old man flinched as the windows were covered and darkness filled the room. The African doctor gently took Tembo's shoulder.

'Stand in front of the machine.' Tembo was as still as a rock. Again came the hiss of the X-ray. The screen came to life and you could see the boy's bones, his chest, his ribs, his spine. A slight movement and there was his heart beating and then his lungs were in focus. We looked at them carefully.

From the back of the room came old Madole's awed voice. 'It is a skeleton - this is witchcraft!' And then he gasped, 'Oh my leg - oh my leg!'

'Quietly!' said the African Medical Officer. He moved the screen again. Tembo's ribs seemed to be moving up and down as I heard a little chuckle and his voice said, '*Heeh*! The old one has fear.'

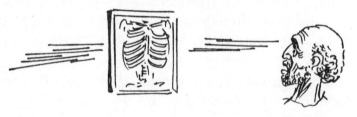

'Yes,' agreed the African doctor, 'and you behaved with courage. But the news is good - you have been greatly helped by the medicines.' He turned to me. 'Why not let him out of bed for an hour or two each day?' He smiled inquiringly at Tembo. 'Would you like that?'

The boy's face was one huge smile. He looked up at me. 'Bwana, will you agree?'

I nodded. 'Now sit in the small room out there with Mboga and think thoughts of joy.'

Again the room was in darkness and a small light was switched on as Madole's stretcher was carried over towards the X-ray machine.

I spoke with firmness. 'Well now, Great One, what is your choice? First though, see your trouble, see what is happening in your own leg and then if you wish our help we will give it to you.'

The light went out. There was the subdued hiss of the X-ray. The old man was propped up so that he could see. The screen before him was alive and green. You could see his leg and the bones, jaggedly broken, the two pieces pointing in different directions. His eyes stared wildly at them, his face ghostly in the pale light.

'Is that my leg? Are those my bones?'

'*Eheh* - and you can see they will never grow together by themselves.'

The old man drew in his breath, 'Help me! Help me! Mend it for me!'

The small light flashed on again.

'We will do that for you, but you understand that to do this would cause great pain, and unless you have the medicine that brings sleep the work cannot be done.'

'*Yoh-heeh*!' said the old man, 'I hate pain, I hate pain! Take it from me - help me!'

'Is it your wish that we do this?'

'*Eheh*! *Eheh*! - help me!'

The next minutes were packed with action. In that airless room we struggled with a difficult surgical task. We were all drenched in sweat when the bones at last came into place. My African medical colleague said, 'He can't stand much more anaesthetic, doctor.'

'All I want is a moment or two to put on a plaster.'

'We can safely do that - plaster sets like concrete in minutes out here. That's one advantage of the tropics.'

The X-ray was switched off, the windows thrown open, the plaster put on and the old man, still asleep, was carried in the stretcher towards the Landrover.

Tembo was sitting in a chair with his eyes nearly popping out. Mboga came across to me and said urgently, 'Bwana, as we sat here we saw Juma come noiselessly down the road. He put this…' In his hand was a long piece of clear plastic tape with black gritty stuff sticking to it. He pushed it into my hands. 'Hide it, Bwana - let no one see it.'

I raised my eyebrows. 'Daudi, look at this - what is it? *Mahala matitu* - black magic?'

'Yes, Bwana,' Daudi nodded. 'That is exactly what it is. And the worst sort. That stuff will kill many men as surely and as swiftly as a sharp knife or a bullet.'

'What is it?'

'A special medicine of deadly poison to men's minds. It is made from the burnt-up bowels of a snake or from the heart of a crocodile. When you see that stuff spread across your doorstep you know what it means - death! If old Madole had seen that he would probably have died before we arrived back at the hospital.'

'But in these days, Daudi, these days of education, surely it's different?'

'Perhaps the fear is a little deeper down, but it is still there.'

'Then tell me - why is it that you, Daudi, and you, Mboga, didn't fear to handle this stuff?'

Mboga grinned. 'I don't like doing it, Bwana, any more than I like touching a snake, but I don't fear. Black magic is of the devil but I am one of God's family. When I was one of *shaitan's* slaves I had reason to fear him - but ever since Jesus rooted the sin out of my life and God forgave me, I have had the strong hand of God protecting me.'

Daudi nodded. 'We really believe this thing. They are not just words, Bwana - they are built into our lives. Do we not prove it by handling the stuff?'

We carried the old man and put him in the back of his station-wagon. Suliman came staggering up. He had occupied his time in Dodoma by a visit to the beer market. I took one look at him and said, 'We will carry Madole back in our Landrover.'

'I pro...protesht...' said Suliman thickly. He took a step forward, tripped and fell. He sat up and looked at us stupidly as we drove off.

'*Koh*!' muttered Mboga. 'Look at that!'

A man in a red fez had hurried across to Suliman. He ran his hand along the back of the station wagon, pointed to us and made dramatic movements with his hands. Both of them started talking at once.

'*Oh-heeh*!' said Daudi, speaking in English. 'He has let the cat out of the bag.'

8

Ominous Finger

We pulled up at the hospital and carried a strangely silent old man to the ward. Mali looked a little apprehensive.

'We gave him the anaesthetic, Mali, and set his leg. All should be well. He needs a strong sedative and a lot of sleep. It's been a trying day for him.'

Tembo stepped down from the front seat of the Landrover, and walked a little shakily to Mali. He put out his hands to her and said, 'See? I am better. I am now allowed to walk, Grandmother.'

I couldn't help feeling that even though *Bibi* - Grandmother - was a term of respect, it didn't fit Mali in the least. She was twenty three years old. She smiled and said, 'This is the only place in the world where two Nursing Certificates makes you a grandmother.'

Walking towards the hospital gate, deep in conversation, were Baruti and Yonah.

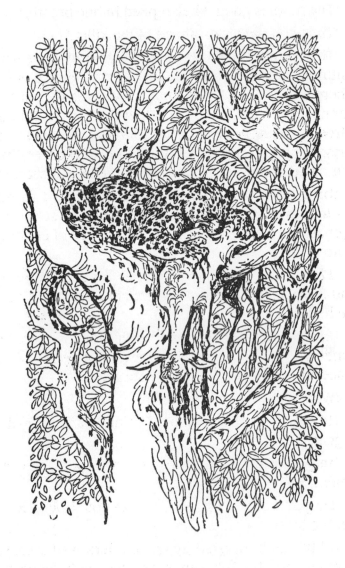

'*Habari*?' I asked.

'The news is good,' they replied in one breath.

'Then you are a step ahead of the killer?'

'That could well be, Bwana. This morning we saw vultures circling high in the air. They led us to a place where leopard had killed a buck. Our eyes helped but our noses brought us to the actual place in the fork of a tree, high above the ground. Such was the light as it passed through the leaves and limbs of the tree that you could barely see leopard lying up there feasting.'

Yonah broke in, 'It is the habit of leopard to put his food high in a tree where it cannot be stolen by hyenas and jackals. But behold, this piece of cunning is no problem to vultures.'

'*Eheh*!,' said Baruti, 'there he was, his eyes glittering and fixed on those birds that circled overhead. If only we had a rifle…'

'*Eheh*,' said Yonah, 'and even now we go. At sundown we will hide where we cannot be seen in a place where the wind blows in our faces.'

'What about your arm, Yonah?'

He shrugged. 'It is stiff but I think I can still pull a trigger.'

'And I,' said Baruti, 'will have my spear and my knife…'

'Do you both feel confident that you'll be able to get the brute?'

A little smile twisted up the corners of the Game Scout's mouth. 'You can never tell with leopards, Bwana.'

'*Yoh-heeh*!' said Baruti. 'Within me I feel that it will

be a night filled with goose pimples!'

The shadows were lengthening as they walked down the hill towards the place where leopard had concealed his kill. Juma's bright yellow Landrover came leisurely up the hill, and stopped outside his house. The two hunters watched him get out, unlock the door, bring out a brightly coloured deck chair and turn on his transistor radio. He had barely tuned it in when the station wagon driven by Suliman came careering up the road and stopped with a screech of brakes. Suliman flung open the door, and jumping to the ground, walked unsteadily towards Juma, who ignored him. Baruti and the Game Scout stopped to see what would happen.

At the top of his voice Suliman yelled, 'I have heard the words of what you did in Dodoma, of the spell that you cast. It is known that you are paid to make medicines against Madole! I am here to warn you that we too work with powerful medicines..!'

Juma's lip curled. 'Shut up, you jackal!'

People started to appear out of the shadows.

'You speak words of no wisdom. The powers of Madole - *kah*! He is old, worn, like a rotten cloth he is torn and tattered. If he can turn himself into a leopard then you no doubt have the power to become a vulture!' A titter ran through those who crowded round. Juma turned to them. 'Listen, Madole has neither the strength of a mouse nor the teeth of an earthworm! And you, Suliman, I warn you. Do not insult leopard lest it turns on you!'

'*Koh*!' said Suliman, spitting, 'I have medicines that protect me from leopards...and liars such as you are!'

Juma ignored this and spoke to the crowd.

'Listen with ears that are wide open. Only my medicines protect. Listen, you people - you will see my strength in the days that come in a way that will bring fear to your hearts. I am one who knows the old ways, yes, and new also.'

The drums started to beat. 'Those of you,' said Juma loudly, 'those of you who have *mapigi* - charms, made by such as this one,' pointing towards Suliman, his voice full of contempt, 'throw them where they belong, in the place of rubbish. Burn them in the fire. Those of you who have the strong ones that I have made, let your mind rest with peace.' He swung round to the Game Scout. 'And you, Yonah Nhuti, why don't you let me make medicines for you which give you power over leopard? Why should people whisper behind their hands that the great hunter has lost his skill, that his heart is melting like beeswax? These are words we hear, is that not so?' There was a nodding of heads from his particular followers. Yonah was tense. He gripped the barrel of his rifle, put the butt of it on the ground and leant forward.

'Your words are empty of meaning, as empty as your medicine is of power!'

Juma straightened his tie. 'Empty of power, you say? When the moon is full you shall see the strength of my medicines. Let each of you watch the moon in the hour after sunset and you will see an event greater than any done by those of older times whose medicines brought rain. You will see the great star that shines without winking, when I order it, hide behind the moon.' He took from the pocket of his safari jacket a yellow lacquered box, opened it, emptied grey powder onto his thumbnail and blew the powder into the air.

There was an awed silence. Juma swung round. 'You, Suliman, toothless jackal of that clawless leopard Madole, you will see the strength of my medicines and the utter weakness of your charms to protect. Watch with eyes that are open and listen with ears that understand!'

Baruti stepped forward and spoke quietly. 'Juma, those who serve the devil and travel his ways have their backs to God. Those with their backs to God travel the ways of darkness which lead suddenly to death. Close your mind to the Lord Jesus Christ and what he has done for you and God's words are: "How will you escape, if you neglect so great a salvation?"'

Juma spat. His voice was heavy with scorn. 'A hunter with empty hands is our Baruti, our man of dynamite. *Heh*! His mouth is full of the words of God! He prays with strength when he faces people. He seems a man of courage. But his brave path never crosses that of leopard! He plays his *ilimba* with skill and no doubt mice tremble when they hear his footsteps.' Juma stopped. There was a cackle of laughter. Cold anger came into the medicine man's voice. From his pocket he took a razor blade and deliberately gashed his index finger and pointed it, dripping blood, at Baruti. 'You speak of death,' he said, 'and so do I! If God protects

you so carefully and loves you so well, make sure he does so now!'

Yonah turned on his heel and he and Baruti walked down the path. The drummer changed his rhythm and people shivered.

When they turned a corner in the road, Yonah said, 'A pointed finger with blood dripping from it - this is witchcraft of the strongest nature. It's an evil thing, a thing of the old ways. Does not fear clutch at your heart?'

Baruti shook his head. 'No, for I remember that the hand of God is stronger than the hand of *shaitan*.'

There was silence till they saw the vultures circling high overhead and crows quarrelling as they tore at the remains of the buck high in the fork of the tall thorntree.

Yonah tested the wind and chose a spot behind a long flat granite outcrop. He whispered to Baruti.' The wind is right and here we can see well behind us and yet we can be seen but little.'

'But what of your damaged arm?' asked Baruti.

'I will lie here and find a place that suits me.'

The sky went from yellow to red to purple. The scavenging birds flew off. At the same instant the keen eyes of both men picked up a movement beyond the tree. Pressing the barrel on the rock in front of him Yonah was looking down the sights.

Barely louder than breathing Baruti whispered, 'To the east of the great buyu tree - see?'

Yonah's head moved a fraction. His finger tightened over the trigger and squeezed. There was a loud report, the whine of a bullet, a grunt from Yonah. 'Missed! *Koh*! How stiff is this arm of mine!'

And then from in front of them came the long-drawn howl of a hyaena.

Yonah grinned, 'Well, that's that. If *Mbisi* the hyaena is here leopard certainly is not! Hyaena has no joy in the anger of leopards. Let us return to the hospital and try again tomorrow.'

In the darkness they walked up the hillside to the hospital, Yonah using his powerful electric torch to probe each bush and tree with light.

I joined them. '*Habari*.'

Yonah spat and then grinned at me. 'The news is good but as empty as a broken eggshell.'

'Come to the hospital. And you, Baruti. There is work there for your music.'

9

Monkey Spot

'What we need above all things tonight, Bwana,' said Daudi, 'is light. We want lamps that bring light, many of them. The place seems so full of darkness and danger and fear clutches at the hearts of the people - a fear of witchcraft, a fear of leopards.'

Soon the hospital was an island of light in the darkness. Outside the wards squatted Yonah, his rifle beside him. But in the middle of things was Baruti, playing his *ilimba*. 'Come,' he cried, 'remind your hearts and your minds that you may have confidence in God, the one whom we call our Father. Don't let fear make you forget that he is the Almighty One. Let us sing, "What a friend we have in Jesus, all our sins and griefs to bear; what a privilege to carry everything to God in prayer..."'

When they had finished singing Baruti said, 'It would be useful now if we talked to God and asked him to help us to overcome this dangerous creature.'

He prayed and when he finished he said, 'There is always a fight going on: God and all that is good against *shaitan* the devil and all that is evil. *Shaitan* and those that work for him prefer darkness. It suits their ways. But we here...' He swept his hand around to the lanterns, '...we look for light, we feel safe in light, we can see where we are going. This is a thing of great importance. Jesus says, "I am the light of the world".'

He pulled his Bible from his pocket, 'And this book says of itself that it is, "a lamp to our feet and a light to our path".'

Baruti smiled around at everybody. 'You feel safe sitting here. Which of you would prefer to walk out there in the dark?' There was a shaking of heads.

'*Eheh*! Leopard reminds you of the danger tonight. Remember this when the whispers of *shaitan* suggest you walk the ways of darkness. Listen, I would tell you the story of the four monkeys...'

Baruti walked into the middle of the courtyard.

'Four small monkeys sat upon a great rock and talked of leopards. The first was somewhat fat and his mouth was large. He said with a yawn, "I have a good way of dealing with leopards. I tell myself they do not exist. I stop thinking of them and contentment comes to my mind."

'Second small monkey had a cunning shape to his face. With scorn in his monkey voice he said, "But they do exist - and they do eat monkeys! Your way is no good at all. Now I have a way of wisdom. Round my neck is a piece of vine. In it is a special thing that keeps me safe from leopards." Very pleased with himself, he looked round at his companions.

'But the third monkey said, "I have a better way than that. In our buyu tree is a lovely big hole that exactly fits my head. I push my head into that hole right up to my neck. I cannot see leopards or hear leopards. I am safe!"

'Fourth monkey had a superior look and a superior sound in his voice. "*Eheh*! I have a better way still. In my buyu tree is a hole just big enough for me to get into and fit into. When I'm in there leopard cannot see me, I cannot see leopard, all is well. There is no problem!"'

Amongst those that listened some chuckled, some looked sideways at one another but the hunter went on...

'One day leopard stalked through the jungle with hunger in his stomach and in his mind a strong desire to eat monkeys. He saw first little monkey on a rock in the sun looking at

nothing at all and thinking thoughts which had not even the shadow of leopards in them.

'Little monkey would have been only a memory if his Uncle Nyani had not thrown a baobab fruit with great accuracy. It caught him in the back of the head, it opened his eyes and his feet did the rest.

'Leopard went on further into the jungle and he saw another of the monkeys. But this monkey also saw him and rushed up his family tree, wedged his head into the hole and sat there with his heart pounding. Somehow his confidence in this  way of safety seemed a thing of small strength when actual leopards were about. *Kumbe*! His heart would have ceased to pound forever if his Uncle Nyani had not moved faster through the trees than leopard could over the ground. With a terrific tug the larger monkey pulled the smaller one from the hole in the tree and swung him high and uncomfortably to safety. Leopard stared at him with cold, hungry eyes...'

'*Yoh*! Great One,' came Tembo's voice, 'but you have forgotten about the monkey that had the vine round his neck.'

'No,' said Baruti, looking at the charm which stood out clearly against the chocolate-coloured skin of a man directly in front of him. 'When that small monkey saw leopard, sudden strength came to his legs and he disappeared into the deeper portions of the jungle. For as the huge, evil beast approached he decided not to trust, after all, in the thing hung round his neck since it was in fact nothing more than an ornament. The only sensible action to take was to put as much distance between himself and the leopard as he could while there was still time.

'Leopard moved on, his nose suddenly telling him the delicious fact that a monkey meal awaited him in the great buyu tree. He climbed by huge leaps and stopped at the hole in the trunk. He looked this way and that and moved himself so that his paw was able to scoop inside the hole.

'When he saw the claws coming towards him little monkey in the hole in the tree howled with fear and would very soon have been the answer to leopard's appetite if Nyani had not thoughtfully pushed over a bees' nest which burst wide open on the limb where leopard crouched - an incident which distracted him not a little!'

Baruti looked at Mboga. A chuckle went round in the lamplight. The hunter waited for it to settle, and then spoke quietly.

'Remember all of you that leopards do exist, that leopards do damage, that leopards do kill. But deadlier than leopards is sin. You can't ignore it, you can't blind yourself to it, you can't hide from it and any sort of charm is useless.'

On the night air came the screaming of the African alarm signal. Yonah picked up his rifle, Baruti his spear and people scuttled indoors.

Mwendwa came rushing through the door. 'In here! Quickly - a light!'

Daudi grabbed a lantern and we hurried through the door. There was a scuffle, a bump and a muttered curse. Madole, screaming in fear, was sitting up wild-eyed in bed trying to protect himself with a pillow. A short broad-shouldered man with a long scar on his scalp was brandishing a knobbed stick.

I ran forward. He saw me coming, brought the stick down with a resounding bang on Madole's plaster-covered leg and dived through the mosquito wire of the window. There was the sound of ripping cloth and a yell of anguish.

Baruti and Mboga burst out laughing and Daudi grinned and said, '*Kah*! What a thing of unexpected joy! Outside that window is a heap of barbed wire and beyond it a pile of thornbush. Then he exclaimed with satisfaction. 'Look, there is blood.'

I could see little but without any trouble he and Baruti followed the trail which disappeared near Juma's house. The door was locked but from within came the sound of a radio at full blast.

'*Kah*!' said Daudi, 'we will certainly not find this man of violence in there. Juma's too cunning for that. This whole affair will become clear as time goes on.'

Before going to bed I visited Tembo. He had coped splendidly with an exhausting day.

Madole had been given a heart pill. He was lying exhausted and speechless. Carefully I tested the plaster. Daudi looked questioningly.

'It's all right. It's dented but no real damage has been done. Isn't it wonderful to have this ward quiet again!'

'*Humph*!' said Daudi. 'There are still three nights to the full moon!'

10
Charmed Death

Early the next morning people from all over the countryside, armed with spears, knobbed sticks and some with rifles and shotguns walked in the direction of Juma's house. Under his baobab tree he sat at a table with a gramophone playing record after record while he did considerable business.

'*Habari,*' said Baruti to a woman who was walking past.

'*Koh*!' she said, 'the news is good. The *muganga* is making *mapigi* of great strength to protect us from leopard. See?' About her neck was the charm that she had just bought for ten shillings. It was made

of yellow and black plastic with a neat bulge in the middle containing the special medicine. This was kept in place by coloured plastic tape.

'*Yoh*!' grunted Yonah. 'Wear it if you must but stay within your house at night!'

Baruti grinned at him. 'What do you think about charms, Yonah?'

The Game Scout grinned. 'The best medicine of all for leopards comes with speed down the barrel of my rifle!'

An old man went past. '*Yoh-heeh*! Did you hear the words of the *muganga* Juma? He says that the charm is so strong that it is as though you were surrounded by a strong thorn bush fence…'

'*Koh*!' said Baruti, 'they believe him, you know.'

'*Eheh*!' said Yonah, 'and worse, they walk outside in the times of darkness with confidence…' He stopped, and fingered his rifle lovingly. 'When it comes to the deadliness of beasts I have confidence in this rifle. Down its sights I have seen the waving trunk and the flapping ears of an elephant maddened by the wounds of ivory poachers. The eye of an elephant is a small target, but the bullet travelled exactly! *Heeh*! And what sight can bring more fear than that of a huge rhino charging with head down!'

'*Kumbe*! said Baruti, 'and you pressed the trigger with confidence?'

'*Eheeh*!' agreed Yonah, 'the bullet did its work.'

'Completely?'

Yonah looked down the sights of the rifle and replied with satisfaction, 'Completely.'

'Listen to my riddle then. There is a creature more deadly than rhino, more violent than elephant, more vicious than leopard and with teeth sharper than crocodile. The most powerful bullet passes right through it doing no damage. Plunge the sharpest knife into it and you draw no blood...'

Yonah looked at him quizzically. '*Koh*! You refer to some disease due to some small germ, *heh*?'

Baruti nodded slowly. 'Almost right. I refer to the worst disease of them all. Have you ever felt pain?'

'*Eheh*!' He looked down at his arm, took it out of the sling and stretched it gingerly.

'The disease in my riddle causes pain. Have you suffered misery?'

'It causes that too. Have you tasted the hollowness of despair?'

Yonah looked up sharply. 'Once - it was a thing of no joy!'

'It is all the work of this disease and death is always at the end of it.'

Yonah stopped, put the stock of his rifle on the ground and said, 'What is the name of this disease?'

'*Hongo*!' said Baruti quietly, 'the name is that given to it by the Great One himself - Almighty God. He calls it sin. He says, "Sin always pays its servants and the wage is death!" But God gives everlasting life. *Kumbe*! You can be confident in God. When he says a thing you can believe it. When he promises you know he will do it, that is, if you keep your part of the bargain.'

'*Heh*! said Yonah, 'I ask him for things when I am in trouble.'

Baruti nodded, 'Many do that, but God is not a Game Scout to be called in emergencies to free you from wild beasts. He wants you to ask him to come into the house of your life. Then he will forgive the punishment that you deserve for your sinning. He promises that, if we become his sons, he will give us an arm strong enough to deal with this death-producing misery-maker, sin.'

Yonah started to stride down the path and as Baruti followed he said, 'I know these words give you small comfort. You trust your rifle, yes, but your arm - is it strong enough? Was it not wounded badly? Did you not miss last night?'

Yonah stopped, faced him, motioned with his chin towards a dead tree two hundred metres away. High on it, silhouetted against the sky, was a vulture. With one incredibly quick action, Yonah lifted the rifle, sighted it and fired. Three other vultures flapped into the air but the one that had been Yonah's target fell like a stone.

'*Heeh*!' said the Game Scout, 'my arm is a little stiff perhaps...' He grinned.

Late in the afternoon Yonah took his arm out of the sling and moved it gingerly up and down.

'*Yoh*!' he said. 'It is stiff. But if I move it a little it becomes less.'

'*Eheh*,' said Baruti, 'each day it heals a little. Try your finger. Does it move with strength...? With enough strength to squeeze a trigger?'

Yonah moved his right finger first, carefully watching each joint. 'You saw me this morning - did I miss then?'

Baruti smiled. 'This is now the hour before sunset - stiffness will mean slowness and slowness can mean jerking of triggers and at the best of times leopards are hard to kill. If you shoot with an arrow, the heart is the place - but behold, who can wait for leopard to turn so that you can shoot at its left side?'

Yonah looked down at the weapon in his hands. 'It is different with a rifle. But even then I have seen one of these great deadly cats travel twenty paces after a bullet has ploughed into its heart! They say that the shot into the eye is the quickest and safest.'

Baruti thought of the difficulty of that particular target, remembering that a centimetre to one side could mean the bullet deflected by the skull of a leopard.

Yonah was carefully testing the wind. He selected a place different from their previous hide and squatted down to wait. With sunset the crows flew overhead and then came the wild cackle of guinea fowl. For a while there was the chirping of crickets and then came mosquitoes.

'*Koh*!' muttered Baruti. 'Yonah, you and I fight the smaller battle against the big creatures. They tell me that for every one person killed by the wild creatures of the jungle, ten thousand die from the bite of mosquito.' He swatted accurately and silently.

With infinite patience they sat with eyes probing the darkness.

'*Yoh*!' said Yonah. 'One more night to the full moon.'

The moon rode through the skies. A mass of cloud came up from the west.

'*Koh*!' grunted Yonah, 'this will make it more difficult. A storm comes and perhaps rain!'

'*Kah*!' said Baruti, 'and look at that…'

Two great yellow eyes far away stabbed into the darkness throwing a beam of light fifty metres ahead of them.

'There goes one we mustn't shoot. Perhaps it is the doctor driving out to collect some sick person.'

A gust of wind blew up and they could hear the throbbing of drums round the villages. Yonah's face twisted into a grin that had no humour in it.

'That row will keep the leopard away from the villages anyhow.'

The cloud swept across the moon. It was quite dark. The headlights of the vehicle could be seen moving in the distance. They swung sharply to the left.

'*Eheh*!' said Baruti, 'they do not go into Dodoma but rather to the great road that stretches from the top to the bottom of Africa.'

'Look up there,' said Yonah, 'things are happening at the hospital all right. Lights are everywhere!' He was moving his shoulder to keep stiffness from coming into it but his grip on the rifle never relaxed. He was holding the weapon so as to be ready for any leopard attack. Baruti's spear was held firmly in his hand.

'*Kah*!' mused Baruti, 'there is no risk of our falling asleep tonight!'

Thunder rumbled in the distance. The moon came and went and in its light their eyes searched for leopard. Far out across the hills a grey curtain seemed to have sprung up between earth and the clouds.

'*Hongo*!' said Yonah, 'it rains with strength over there.'

'*Eheh*,' agreed Baruti, 'and when that happens the rivers run. If that is the doctor we saw it would be a thing of small joy to him if his machine sticks in the soft sand of the dry river, for behold, before the night is much older, that dry sand will be under a metre of tossing red water, as angry as any rhino!'

The storm came closer. The sky was cracked with jagged lightning. The country seemed to come and go with each flash. A new sound of strident singing reached them.

'*Yoh*!' said Yonah, 'trouble. Someone has filled his stomach with beer and because of this his wisdom has become small.'

Baruti pointed with his chin. 'The sound comes from over there. Behold, that one's danger is great. Here we have weapons. Away beyond the hospital they have light and drums that bring wariness to a leopard.

But in between, *yoh*! It is the place any leopard would rejoice to hunt!'

Forked lightning gave them a black-and-white picture of the African hillside behind them. Silhouetted starkly was the figure of a stocky man.

'*Heeh*!' said Yonah, 'it is the one who attacked Madole last night. Behold, do you not see the pattern? He has today received money from Juma for his work and turned that money into beer…'

'*Heeh*!' went on Baruti, 'and the beer has so reduced his wisdom that he is little better than bait for a leopard…' As he spoke, a picture of what it could mean came into his mind. A cold shudder moved slowly up his spine.

Darkness pressed down on them. Again the lightning flashed and in that second they saw the staggering figure waving his arms and, rising to meet him, the lithe figure of leopard. The thunder crashed but as it died away came a shrill terrified scream.

Yonah was on his feet, with Baruti close behind him, flashing a strong electric torch over his shoulder. They broke into a run. Rain came down in torrents so that they could see only a few paces ahead of them. At last they stood before the crumpled body of Juma's strong-arm man.

'It is he,' grunted Yonah, 'see that long scar? *Kah*! What a blow that brute gave him.'

Leopard had killed with one blow.

Baruti picked the man up, putting him over his shoulder. Then they turned and forced their way back through the storm.

As they neared the hospital it was obvious there were unusual goings-on. Yonah came to me.

'Bwana, Baruti stands in the shadow of the great buyu tree. He has with him a man who is dead.'

'It isn't Madole, is it?'

'No, Bwana. Is he not here in bed?'

'No, he has disappeared and with him that Suliman. They drove away in what looked like panic. Do you think they were dodging Juma's spells?'

Yonah nodded. 'We have brought in the one who yesterday attacked Madole with a knobbed stick. On his legs, his hands and his face are the scars left by the barbed wire and the thornbush - but he is dead. We saw it happen. The bones of his neck were crushed by the paw of leopard, crushed as you would bend a corn stalk.'

In the pathology room it became clear to me that the man had died within seconds of the leopard attack. He was beyond medical aid of any sort.

Daudi lifted the yellow plastic charm which had been driven deep into the skin by the force of the leopard's blow.

'This should answer those who have faith in *mapigi*. Behold how utterly futile it is to have faith in the wrong thing!'

'*Hodi.*' At the door of my office was Baruti dressed in some of Mboga's clothes. 'What has happened, Bwana?'

'Everything seems to have happened tonight! First came twins - and that was work. And then, when everyone was busy helping in an emergency transfusion, Suliman came into the ward. He lifted Madole in his arms and carried him out to their station wagon. On the way he took a bottle of pills from the table, the pills he thought were for heart attacks, but not reading the label was a mistake for he only stole the small pills that we use for those whose stomachs are uneasy. Before we could do anything they had driven away.'

'*Eheh*!' said Mboga, 'with two of our blankets, two of our pillows and with no thankfulness in their hearts!'

A slow smile came over Baruti's face. 'I can see a way of no joy before those two. We saw their station wagon drive off. They have travelled the road away from Dodoma! They must cross the wide rivers where flooding is happening at this minute. Madole himself has no strength and a leg supported by plaster…'

I broke in, 'He has a heart that has small usefulness as hearts go and when violent pain comes, as it will through this excitement, he has only the wrong pills to help him.'

Mboga was unusually serious. 'Bwana, you will never understand the terror of death that comes into the minds of the people of this country when they come up against black magic such as Juma has made. This was not bad at the beginning but now they have no confidence in the charms they wear and they bolt for their lives. They turn their backs on God. He could change everything for them if they would turn to him.'

Baruti nodded. 'If we turn our backs on the things that are wise, helpful and right - *kumbe*! We find only trouble!'

'*Yoh-heeh*!' said Mboga, 'and as you told me the

other day, the words of God in this matter are: "Be sure your sin will find you out".' He turned to see if his words had made an impression on Yonah.

Yonah was crouched in his chair. Sweat was pouring from his forehead and he was shivering.

'Bwana,' he muttered, 'fever grips me...'

11
Full Moon

'*Kumbe*!' said Daudi, 'the night of the full moon is ahead of us.'

'That may be, but between now and sunset is a day of much work. A message must be sent to the police regarding the man killed by leopard last night... Yonah's attack of fever is no ordinary one... We must keep a watchful eye on young Tembo... There are six eye operations to do...'

'*Eheh*! And also, a man has arrived with a great swelling in his face - a tooth in his jaw which he calls an enemy.'

'I have looked at it and I feel that even if you had the strength of the trunk of an elephant in your wrist it would take much effort to move that molar.'

The storm had turned the countryside into a sea of red mud.

I wrote a letter to the African Inspector of Police and said to the bus driver, 'Gideon, do you think you will get through?'

'Yes, doctor,' he grinned. 'We may skid in the mud but we will not stick in the sand. Even if we do we will not find it dull now that I have the radio. It gives me joy to hear music and *kumbe*! The news comes three times a day. These days the world's doings come right into my bus. *Kwaheri* - good-bye!' He let in his clutch.

As Mali came hurrying out of the ward she called, 'Bwana, will you come and see Yonah. His temperature has shot up.'

Four blankets covered an unhappy Game Scout.

'Bwana, sickness grips me. My head throbs. My chest aches and my back feels as though it were beaten by hippo-hide whips.'

He set his jaws as his teeth started to chatter. We took a drop of blood from his finger and an hour later the report was back - heavy malarial infection. The hunter looked at me with a troubled face. 'This is an evil thing.'

'Uncomfortable, Yonah, and it means bed. No more leopard-hunting for you for days.'

'*Kah*!' he muttered. 'I have no joy, not even a little bit.'

Daudi walked with me to the children's ward.

114

'It is a matter of thankfulness that Baruti is here. *Kumbe*! These days he is a changed person. Four years ago they called him Baruti - dynamite - because of his temper. When I heard the words of Juma yesterday I thought, *yoh*! There was a time not long ago when those words would have caused a bitter fight. I marvelled that Baruti stayed calm and quiet.'

'What do you think made the difference, Daudi?'

'He has been a different man from the day he heard the words of God here in the hospital. He believed them and started going God's way.'

'What do you think Juma is up to?'

'He says he has a special thing of wonder to show them at nightfall.'

Juma, the medicine man, sat in a brightly coloured deck chair outside his house. He contrived to be aloof from the crowd of people who stood silently some twenty metres away gazing at a folding table on which there were a number of vessels and bottles and jars. People whispered expectantly but Juma sat watching the sun setting like a great ball of fire.

More and more people were coming towards his house. The drums were beating to keep the leopard away from the village. A furtive-looking man came hurrying down the path from the hospital. He stood at a respectful distance and said, '*Hodi*?'

Without a word Juma beckoned him to approach. In a husky whisper the messenger said, 'Bwana Juma, at the hospital there is consternation. Yonah Nhuti, the Game Scout, has been struck with a great fever. They crowd around his bed. I think he's dead. Surely your medicines have strength beyond words.'

Juma smiled coldly, dismissed the man with a gesture and moved across to the table. He put a long-playing record of drums on his transistorised gramophone, turned up the volume and then sat down, his face mask-like as he waited for his big moment to arrive.

Darkness came quickly. He stood to his feet and pointed dramatically towards the horizon.

'See, the moon rises. Watch it with alert eyes. Watch also the sky as it turns from blue to black. You have all seen me make medicine. You will never see a thing of greater strength or wisdom or power than this. Let your eyes convince you that this is a thing that you will be able to tell your children's children. This is a medicine of strength never yet seen in this country or in any part of the whole of Africa. Fix your eyes upon the great star that does not wink. Watch it.'

A thousand eyes in that grove of baobab trees were fixed on the moon and that very bright planet.

As darkness became deeper it seemed that the star was moving fast towards the moon. In a deep voice that he threw high into the air Juma addressed the planet.

'There is no call for hurry. Travel with certainty and hide behind her.'

There was an awed silence then a young woman with rolling eyes who was standing astride a drum started to beat it. She began to sing in a voice that sounded as though she had been hypnotised. Her theme was taken up and tongues trilled. More drums took up the rhythm. Juma stood, his hands raised, still as an image. Among the crowd there were a number who looked at one another with fear.

'*Yoh*!' came a voice. 'This will surely bring disaster upon us.'

'*Eheh*!' said another. 'This is witchcraft of a sort never yet heard of.'

Juma turned and blew on a whistle. There was immediate silence. 'Have no fear,' he said, 'I will free the star even as I have caused the moon to clutch it and hold it.' He opened his yellow-enamelled box ornamented with black stars. He took from it a package, opened it, and onto the palm of his hand he poured some bright yellow powder.

'Bring fire,' he ordered. A dish of glowing charcoal was brought.

'Before I use the medicine that will bring this star back,' he cried, 'listen to my words. I, Juma bin Ali, have the answer not only to the things of everyday, but behold, when there are those who travel the dangerous path of *wuchawi* - witchcraft, and when their path has crossed yours…' He paused, and looked around from face to face. People shrank back a step. 'Remember that I, Juma, have the answer. Everybody knows that sickness comes because of the ill-will of another. We all know the hostility of spirits.' He glanced at his gold wrist-watch. 'These things we do not speak openly, but tonight it is different. You shall see how I shall free the star from the power of the moon. One who can do a thing of this sort can free a man from the medicines of his evil-wishers as a lion would crush a frog.'

'*Yoh*!' came a quavering voice. 'My blood turns to water.'

'*Eheh*,' came the reply, 'this is strange witchcraft of a terrible sort.'

Juma had paused and the man's voice, low as it was, was distinctly audible.

Juma smiled, 'We are not speaking of witchcraft,' he purred - but he managed to convey an utterly different meaning.

In the shadows of the baobab tree two other men spoke.

'*Yoh*! His medicines have the power to kill. Think of the man whose neck the leopard broke last night.'

Again Juma glanced at his watch. Nineteen minutes had passed since the planet had been swallowed up by the full moon. Juma took two gourds, the traditional gear of a medicine man. Into one he tipped the yellow powder, into the other he emptied a bottle. The air reeked of methylated spirits. Dramatically he threw the yellow powder on the glowing coals. There was blue flame and a cloud of pungent smoke. Stepping further back, he threw the contents of the second gourd. A sheet of flame shot up. The people staggered backwards and fell over one another. Juma poured what was left in the gourd over his arm, moving it towards the flames. It was as though the fire leapt onto his arm and blue flame flickered there before going out. There were screams of fear and gasps of amazement. The smell of burning sulphur made people cough and choke. Juma jumped in the air and at the top of his voice yelled, 'You may come from behind her!'

Every eye turned towards the moon. A speck of light seemed to appear at one side and then a great roar came from hundreds of throats.

'He has freed it! He has freed it!'

We heard that roar at the hospital half a mile away. Everyone well enough to be out of bed was standing watching the night sky.

Daudi had placed the radio in the middle of the court-yard and for the last half-hour the people crowded round the wireless set, thrilled, as the eclipse had been described and explained. As Venus appeared again on the far side of the moon, an African scientist, speaking in Swahili, said, 'Here in Dar-es-Salaam we have seen the eclipse splendidly. Weather conditions were ideal…' He went on to talk about astronomy and rockets to the moon.

Tembo stood up and stretched. '*Hongo*! Listen how they beat drums down by the buyu trees!'

Mboga came at the double from that direction. He panted, '*Yoh*! Down there Juma has brought amazement and terror into many hearts. He says that he can control the moon.'

'*Koh*!' said Daudi. 'He is a fraud, a liar and a cheat!'

'That's true, Daudi, but he's clever. Did he not say that Yonah would be hit by fever? He knew that the Game Scout's country is far from here and the brand of malaria is a different one. Now, sitting out there waiting for leopards is the best way I know to feed mosquitoes and collect a brisk attack of fever.'

'*Kumbe*!' grunted Mboga, 'those who live his way and do the things he does always say, "What are a few lies or a few lives if you can make money?"'

Daudi turned off the radio. 'Listen - in the Bible are these words: "The heavens declare the glory of God, and the firmament shows his handiwork." We have been watching the moon and the stars. Look at the way they move - certainly, punctually. An eclipse like the one we have seen can be predicted years and years before it happens. Our eyes can't see God himself but we can see the way his hand works.'

'It was in the beginning that God made the heavens and the earth and he made man of the same pattern as he is himself and he gave everybody freedom to travel the way that he would choose. God said, "Go my way and you will find life and peace and happiness and usefulness and adventure".'

From outside came the rumble of Gideon's bus. A door slammed and the driver came up to us. '*Habari*?'

'*Koh*!' said Daudi. 'The place is alive with news.'

The driver grinned. 'And I carry even more. Did you see the eclipse?'

'We did, indeed.'

'Down there,' said Mboga, pointing with his chin towards the baobab tree grove, 'Juma has been telling very many people that he has power to influence the stars.'

'*Hongo*!' laughed Gideon, 'many people will cease to believe that when they hear the words of the wireless.'

Baruti chuckled. '*Koh*! Things are hard for medicine men these days.'

'There you spoke truth,' said Gideon, 'things are hard for medicine men. Did you hear what happened to Madole and that young man of many words who goes with him?'

'All we know is that last night they drove away from here in fear of the medicines of Juma, but they were still capable of stealing some bedclothes and some medicine.'

'*Kumbe*! My news is much later. They travelled some small way down the Great North Road and then, behold, they skidded. I met one who told me that he saw the machine lying on its back with its wheels in the air like a tortoise in distress.'

'*Hongo*! And what happened to Madole?'

'He is in Dodoma Hospital. I heard his voice raised in loud complaint.'

'And what about the person who calls himself Doctor Suliman?'

Gideon grinned broadly. 'That I thought was amusing. He arrived at the hospital, demanded to see the doctor at once and when he did his words were these: "My arm is damaged - I demand X-rays - and then for the setting of the bones I also demand that I be given an anaesthetic".'

Daudi rolled his eyes, '*Yoh*! Well at least we taught him something!'

12
Goat Bait

Mboga handed Tembo his pills.

'Swallow them with speed, Little Elephant,' he chuckled, 'that they may bring misery to the germs which live with so little peace within your skin. *Kumbe*! I wonder if they are finding life as difficult today as does Juma the medicine man.'

Daudi grinned, 'I hear that people keep coming to him and asking why it is that the man who was killed by the leopard was not protected by the charm which he had round his neck.'

Mboga broke in, 'And others say the word moves through the villages that they heard on the wireless days ago that the moon would cover up the bright star.'

'Truly,' said Baruti, 'the faith of many wobbles a little in the work of that young man with the yellow Landrover and the yellow charms.'

'*Kah*!' said Daudi, 'but his skin is thick. Any hippopotamus would be proud to have one like his.'

Tembo sat on the edge of his bed swinging his legs. 'Today is a big day for me. I am going out with Baruti.'

'Go gently, Tembo. And take times of resting,' Mali cautioned. 'If he does not obey these words, Baruti, hit him with your spear in such a way and on such a place that he may remember.'

Baruti smiled down at the boy and said, 'It shall be done.'

They went across to the workshop where the hunter sharpened his axe, tried the edge on his thumb and said, '*Yoh*! Tembo, it is now as sharp as the small knives the Bwana uses at the hospital to mend eyes. Let us go.'

Together they walked down the long winding path behind the hospital, past the nearer baobabs to a clearing almost completely surrounded by thornbush. Not so far beyond it were the taller trees in one of which leopard had concealed his kill.

'This is what we shall do,' said Baruti. 'We will cut long limbs of thorn bush - the longer they are, the stronger they are. We must build an *ibululu* - a fenced-in courtyard. We must build it high so that leopard cannot jump over. We must build it thick so that he cannot push his way through it. Above all, we must build it STRONG. Sit here and I will build a model out of twigs…'

In the dust he traced a rough circle and weaved the thornbush into a miniature hedge. He pushed his thumb underneath it.

'Here there will be the entrance, just wide enough for you to crawl through and just wide enough for leopard to do the same.'

Tembo's eyes sparkled with excitement. 'But will leopard come to the place? And how are you going to cause him to walk into it? And when he does walk in what are you going to do to him?'

Baruti laughed. 'This is a way of cunning. For many days I have been watching this leopard and his habits and now I try to think as he thinks. Even now as we talk he is watching us from somewhere. Every hunter knows that for every animal he sees in the jungle ten see him!' He spat on his hands, picked up the axe and cut a pile of thick poles. He sharpened them and then started driving these strong stakes into the ground. Two of the largest, not quite a metre apart, were directly facing the hospital.

Looking through the ward window Mboga said to Mwendwa, 'Behold, Baruti and the boy are working in the far clearing.'

'*Hongo*!' said Mwendwa, who was bandaging a man's leg, 'what are they doing?'

'Baruti chops limbs from thorntrees and Tembo piles them up. They are building an *ibululu*.'

'*Kumbe*!' said the African nurse, 'Baruti does nothing without a plan behind it. He is a man of wisdom.'

'Truly,' agreed Mboga, 'and did he not sit here for an hour this morning with a great nail and a file until he made that nail grow sharp as an injection needle. And then he put deep grooves along its side...'

Mwendwa carefully tied the bandage. '*Mmm*, and I heard him talking to the doctor and asking what strong poisons we have and which work fastest.'

Mboga rolled his eyes. '*Koh*! Baruti is a man full of deep schemes.'

Down in the clearing Baruti had just chopped through a thornbush and was lopping off great limbs. Suddenly he grunted, dropped the axe and hobbled over into the shade.

'*Hongo*!' said Tembo, ' a thorn, Great One? I'll pull it out for you - sit here in the shade.'

He lifted Baruti's foot, took off the cowhide sandal and then gripped the end of the thorn with his finger-tips. '*Kah*! Don't they hurt!' With a deft movement he pulled out the sharp, iron-hard thorn.

'*Asante - thank you*,' said Baruti, putting his hand on Tembo's shoulder. 'And speaking of thorns, do you remember saying yesterday that you wished God had been a man so that you could understand what he looked like and what he thought?

'God knew people's need in this matter. That's why he came to earth. He was born as you and I are born, he grew. He suffered, he taught people. He healed people. And when he had seen thirty-three harvests, then it was that he suffered greatly for you and me and everybody else everywhere. They whipped him with a lash that tore his skin. They made a crown of thorns and pushed it down on his forehead with hands that had no gentleness in them.'

Tembo shuddered.

Baruti picked up a branch and fingered the two-inch spikes. 'We know how thorns can hurt...but worse was to follow. They drove nails through his hands and feet. They nailed him to a wooden cross. He allowed this to happen to him so that he might have the double medicine to offer us for the disease of our soul.'

'Double medicine?' said Tembo. 'What do you mean?'

'You see, if we ask him, Jesus will forgive us so that we will not be punished for our sins. This is the first great medicine of freedom. And the second one stops sin  from having power in our lives.'

Baruti picked up his axe. 'I must build with speed. Sit here and rest. When I want your help I will call.'

Soon the courtyard surrounded by thornbush had taken shape. Baruti stopped at the place where he had driven in the largest stakes.

'Lie down here, Tembo. I will build the entrance over your body.'

He skilfully made a framework of sticks and as the boy crept forward the narrow passage was built. He picked up two more strong stakes.

'Sit inside here for a moment. I am going to put in a wider place.'

Tembo sat cross-legged and watched. 'Is this the place where leopard will be surprised?'

'It is more than that. It's the place in which I plan to kill him.'

'Kill him? How?'

'See. I tie this stick with a small branch on it to these strong stakes and at about the level where a leopard's knees will pass I tie this piece of string. When he touches it, even lightly, this thin stick is pulled out of the ground, and *pow*! down comes a heavy lump of wood that drives the spike through his skin and lets the strong poison work to bring death to his cruel and dangerous heart.'

'Show me the spike, Baruti.'

The hunter put into his hands a lump of hardwood as thick through as his thigh and half as long. Driven firmly into it was the long sharpened nail, the grooves completely hidden with greasy black material.

'Is that really poison?'

'It is indeed. Don't touch it! It would kill a man as fast as it will kill a leopard. Hold it carefully for me. I have another piece of wood here that I will use for testing.'

He connected this up to the string and adjusted everything with great care.

'It is of high importance, Tembo, that the spike should fall between the shoulders of leopard. Now, let's see if it works.'

With his spear, time and again Baruti tested and

adjusted the trap. Then he nodded, 'It works. Now I will finish the *ibululu*.'

More thornbush was cut and woven into place and soon the whole leopard trap was ready. In the middle of the thornbush enclosure was a post that Baruti fixed firmly into the ground. He knotted a stout rope carefully to it.

'What is that for, Great One?'

'This is the place for the bait of the trap. To this rope I will tie the largest and strongest goat in my herd.'

'*Koh*! The goat will have no joy in that!'

'Truly, but this leopard also is a creature of no joy. It has killed and killed again and it is better for a goat to die than for a man.' He held up the rope. 'Do you not see, the goat will be free to walk about?'

Tembo opened his eyes wide. 'Free, did you say? *Koh*! Free to walk about, truly, but tied to a rope so that it cannot possibly get away! *Yoh*! That isn't really being free...'

Baruti piled more thorns on a thin place and said, 'Small Elephant, you have grasped the all-important point as firmly as you grasped the thorn that was in my foot. There are many people who think that they are free but really they are tied up by their own sins. They are not really free until that rope is gone - and it's being really free that matters more than anything!'

Baruti walked right round the leopard trap, testing it here and there. He nodded with satisfaction. 'It is strong. You are tired. Now come...' He swung the boy onto his shoulders and walked up the path to the hospital.

'Which goat will you use, Great One?'

'The brown-and-white he-goat whose strength is not only in his legs.'

Tembo laughed. '*Heeh*! Leopard's nose need not be sharp to know that he is there!'

As they came near the hospital the hunter said, 'I am relying on you to watch with care through the telescope. If trouble should come, send those who will help.'

'Do you expect trouble?'

'Who can tell?' said Baruti, as he walked off along the path to his house. From his herd he took the goat he had chosen.

There was hardly a person in the whole village who did not watch as he dragged the reluctant goat towards the trap. Tembo had rested the telescope on the window-sill of the men's ward.

'*Hongo*! It is even as though I could put out my hand and touch him! See, he pulls aside the thornbush in the northern corner. It is here that you can get in, but you must know exactly the right branch to pull or it will not move even a little.'

'*Koh*!' said Mboga, 'that goat surely has fear.'

Tembo's voice dropped, '*Eheh*! I can see it in every move it makes. *Yoh!* And it is tied to the post…'

131

Baruti checked the knots carefully and then without hurrying walked to the thornbush hedge, pulled a branch to one side, forced his body through and most carefully repaired and reinforced the spot. As he walked up the hill again he prayed, 'God, help me to catch that brute. But if you think that other bait would be better for the whole plan...' He went on praying but somehow his thoughts did not seem to fit into words.

A kilometre away, standing on the roof of his Landrover and using his field glasses, Juma the medicine man watched and smiled a cynical smile.

From the complete camouflage of shadows behind a great rock the blazing eyes of leopard watched every move.

Mboga murmured to Mwendwa and Tembo, '*Koh*! I'm glad I'm not that goat - death is so close to those who are tied up securely like it is. See, he tugs and strains but no goat can free himself...'

Tembo's eyes were fixed to the telescope but through his head went the words, 'Your sins tie you down. You are not really free...' And he remembered how Baruti had said, 'Sin kills more certainly than any leopard'.

He saw a movement in the deep shadows, focused carefully and gasped as a broad beam of sunlight lit up the lithe yellow killer as he confidently walked into the open. He seemed to say that he knew he was secure and out of rifle shot. His whole poise was of calculated power. The wretched goat saw him coming and broke into terrified bleating as the leopard stopped, facing him through almost a metre of thornbush fence.

There was a tense hush. Tembo could see lips moving everywhere but the whispering was lost in the ordinary sounds of late afternoon.

Yonah, so ill with malaria that he could only stagger, supported himself on Baruti's strong shoulder and groaned, '*Yoh*! If only this fever didn't grip me, if only there was strength in my body…'

'*Kah*!' whispered Mboga, 'I'm praying that he'll walk straight into that narrow passage where death waits for him!'

'So am I,' breathed Tembo.

As though he was conscious that he was in the centre of the stage, leopard crouched in front of the passage-way. Goat cowered back, dragging wildly at the rope. High above, vultures started to circle.

Amongst the far baobabs, Juma stood on the top of his Landrover, his field glasses to his eyes. Beneath him, open-mouthed, were a number of his followers. Crisply he told them what was happening.

'Leopard has come to the trap. He stands before it. He crouches there. He looks into the passage…'

'*Koh*!' came a voice, 'can you see the poisoned spike?'

'No,' said Juma, 'not from here. *Koh*! You should see that goat…' There was a cruel line around his mouth.

'Does the leopard walk into the pathway to death?'

'*Heeh*!' said Juma, 'behold, the great cat stands upon his feet. *Yoh*! Look at those muscles. *Ugh*! He walks slowly round the *ibululu*, his lips are drawn back, he snarls… *Koh*! Goat nearly chokes himself from dragging on that rope…'

Deliberately he put the field glasses down, took from his pocket a small black bottle, tipped some powder from it onto his hand and blew it in the direction of the leopard. The people on the ground below him hastily scuttled out of the way.

'Have no fear,' said Juma, 'that is medicine that will work only on leopards. My words are these: Leopard will die but not through the trap that Baruti has set. My medicine will free you from this leopard, but not by the old ways of thornbush traps baited with goats!'

Still clinging onto Baruti's shoulder at the hospital, Yonah Nhuti, his teeth chattering, said, 'Behold, see, leopard walks round the *ibululu*. He crouches again at the gateway. As clearly as if he used words he is saying to anyone who knows the ways of leopards, "Traps are for animals of small experience, not for one of cunning such as I am".'

'*Eheh*!' said Mboga, 'and I am sure that at this very minute Juma has seen this also - he is more cunning even than leopard. He is telling those who swallow every word that he says that he will make medicine to prevent leopard from going into the trap.'

Tembo muttered to Baruti, 'And I am praying and praying that the leopard will go in and God is taking no notice at all!'

The vultures were circling lower and lower. The goat had fallen and tangled itself in the rope in its frenzy to escape. Leopard looked at it with complete contempt as if to say, 'I am not interested in goats, it is people that I kill.'

With head held high, he stalked back into the jungle and seemed to melt into the shadows as if by magic.

'*Yoh*!' said Baruti. 'Gone!'

'No,' rapped Yonah, 'look - even now he turns and looks back. See him on that great rock!'

Dramatically, *Chewi* was clearly visible again. He looked haughtily in every direction.

Juma cried, 'Behold - my medicine has worked! It has worked with strength. As leopard looked down that narrow passage with its poison spike of death, my medicine opened his mind. He saw. He understood! He looked at the goat with scorn. *Koh*! And goat has behaved in the way of all goats. It has struggled, it has fallen, it lies exhausted and full of terror. *Kah*! And leopard turns and walks away!'

'*Hongo*!' came voices from below him, 'behold, Great One, your medicines have strength!'

'That is indeed so,' said Juma curtly. He climbed down and began a brisk trade in charms.

At the hospital Mboga helped Yonah Nhuti back to bed and said, '*Heeh*! What do we do now?'

Baruti stood up, his eyes gleaming. 'All of you, think of what has happened these last few minutes and look again at goat. Think, what value was his freedom? Is he not tied by a rope that he cannot break to a stake that will not move? Is he not surrounded by a fence so sharp, so thick, so tall, that even if he broke the rope he could not escape? Who, of his own free will, would choose a freedom of that sort?'

He paused and then in a ringing tone continued, 'In the hospital here you and I feel safe, not at all like that wretched animal. But every one of us here is or has been like that goat!'

'*Koh!*' said Yonah, 'what do you mean?'

'We think we are free,' replied Baruti. 'But we think only with the wisdom of goats. We are tethered with a rope that we cannot break to a stake that we cannot pull out.

'What is the name of the rope? I'll tell you - sin - doing the things that we know we should not do. This tethers us.'

'You ask me what is the name of the hedge of thorns that keeps us in - that keeps us from escape? I will tell you that also - again it is sin - not doing things we know we ought to do.'

'Look down there and realise with all your mind that these things are real...'

He stopped suddenly. '*Koh*! It would be a thing of cruelty to leave that goat down there any longer.'

He whipped round on those that looked at him with wide-open eyes. 'And you here, why should you be cruel to yourself and stay tied up and fenced in when you can be really free?' He turned on his heel and strode through the door.

'*Kah*!' gasped Yonah. 'Do not let him go alone! Have you forgotten the leopard?'

But Baruti had already gone.

'Quickly!' shouted the Game Scout. 'Bring me my rifle.' He struggled after his friend, went about two hundred metres and then almost collapsed against a rock. He lay there for a minute and then contrived to prop himself up on his good elbow and lift the rifle so that he could look down its sights.

In the meantime, Baruti had reached the *ibululu*. He pulled out the thornbush which enabled him to enter. He slipped the rope from the goat's neck. The terrified animal bolted for its life, dashing through the gap and careering up the hill to the safety of Baruti's house. Carefully the hunter lifted out the poisoned spike and put the thornbush back into place. He strode back up the hill muttering to himself, 'Truly, there is small joy in being live bait.'

A yell came from the people watching, 'Baruti! Run!'

The last rays of sunlight spotlighted leopard, his mouth open in a snarl. He stood on the trunk of a fallen buyu tree defiantly, making no attempt to follow the hunter.

Yonah fired, and fired again. The leopard took not the slightest notice.

Baruti came at a steady trot up the hill. As he came level Yonah stumbled to his feet.

'*Koh*! It is no good. It is as though that leopard had the mind of *shaitan* the devil within it!'

Underneath the buyu trees Juma whipped round to his followers.

'You, Nungho, run to the hospital and pour out words of scorn about Baruti and Yonah - and do it well!'

13
Man Bait

'*Koh*!' said Yonah. 'Baruti, you will understand. It is as though a spell has been cast against me. As I lay there the rifle would not stay still. My eyes could not hold the sights in line and the leopard himself moved up and down and changed shape in a way that…' He stumbled, dropped his rifle and would have fallen but for Baruti's supporting arm.

Mboga came dashing through the gate and Tembo, feeling most important, picked up the rifle and followed them towards the hospital. They moved slowly, and as they came to outside the men's ward, from the shadows near the pathology room came an odd-looking figure blowing on a kudu horn. He succeeded in getting everyone to look in his direction and then, in a high-pitched voice, he taunted.

'*Yoh-heeh*! So the hunters have returned with empty hands and mouths full of explanations. Baruti will sing hymns and pray large prayers and Yonah will say how sick he feels and how the fever grips him and stops him from shooting straight. Expert hunters indeed - with words…!' He spat disdainfully and tooted on his kudu horn, then shouted, 'Brave, brave Yonah! Brave, brave Baruti!'

There was a grim line round Yonah's mouth but Mboga grinned and said softly, 'Leave it to me. There was one who brought a gift today of ten eggs to the hospital. Eight of them were bad - they floated when I put them in water. But it was a gift of importance and usefulness for a time such as this!'

Three times in quick succession he threw. The dancing figure blowing its odd trumpet had moved further back into the shadows. His musical efforts ended in a sudden 'squawk'.

Daudi shone his torch on the wretched man, who was wiping ancient egg from his face.

Mboga held his nose. '*Kah*! The first one fell short, the second landed at his feet, but the third one - *heeh*! - what a triumph! And it was an egg of small merit, truly.'

A chuckle went round the hospital grounds.

Yonah was put back to bed. Baruti said, '*Kwaheri* - good night!' and walked quietly to his house.

An hour later Mboga came to his door. He held a lantern in one hand and a spear in the other.

'*Hodi*?'

'*Karibu* - come in!'

Mboga pushed open the door and Tembo slipped in behind him. Baruti was sitting on a three-legged stool reading. Mboga, most unlike his usual cheery self, said, 'Bwana Baruti, Tembo here has words within him which he says will not permit sleep till you have heard and answered them.'

Tembo burst out, 'Great One, God didn't answer my prayers! I asked him, very hard indeed, that the leopard would go into that trap, and he didn't do it!'

Baruti smiled. 'I can think of two good reasons why he may not have done what you asked, Small Elephant!' The boy's mouth fell open in amazement.

'*Koh*! But you said that God always listens to us!'

'Truly, he always listens to us, but he doesn't always answer yes to whatever we ask him to do. You see, he may have another way and so he answers no. But the big and important thing is, do you have any right to ask God to do things for you?'

'*Koh*!' said the boy. 'Any right? Why, God made me, didn't he?'

'He did, truly. But this thing that I have been telling you about called sin puts a wall between you and God and that wall must be got rid of before you can expect him to listen to you. But there's always one prayer that gets through to God and if you mean it from the bottom of your heart his answer is always yes...'

'*Koh*!' said the boy, 'and what are these words?'

'I prayed them three years ago when I came to the hospital here with the stabbing disease and first heard about Jesus. They are, "God, please forgive me. Please take away my sin for Jesus' sake".'

'*Hongo*!' said the boy.

Mboga sat absolutely still on his stool, his face expressionless. Tembo looked at him and then across at the door.

Baruti opened his mouth to say something more but changed his mind. He sighed, '*Hongo*! I am glad you have both come, for tonight my mind boils. I must attack that leopard. I've been praying and reading the Bible - these are real ways of action. I've asked God to show me what to do and he has. I have been thinking how King David killed a lion and a bear, and another man of strength called Benaiah went down into a pit and killed a lion on a snowy day. *Koh*! That was a thing of courage! Then there was Samson who killed a young lion with his bare hands. Through these things God has shown me another road that I must travel.'

He stood up and paced up and down. Then he stopped and leaned against one of the uprights of the house. 'I believe the answer is that I must change the bait.'

There was the sound of hurrying footsteps outside. A voice called, '*Hodi*?' and the door was pushed open. Mwendwa bustled in.

'Mboga, run with speed to the doctor's house and bring him at once. Yonah Nhuti is suddenly and dangerously ill. Tell the Bwana that in the last hour Yonah's neck has become stiff, his temperature is 105°, great sickness has come upon him and he has a headache beyond all headaches! Also, his eyes look in different directions.'

A few minutes later Mboga delivered his message and he and I both tried to appear unconcerned on that two-hundred-metre walk to the hospital. As we came close to the ward Mboga's smile grew wider.

'*Yoh*! Behind every blade of grass we have travelled I thought there was a leopard! Behind every tree, a wild elephant, and every patch of shade seemed a venomous snake!'

'*Eheh*! I know how you feel, Mboga. I also had creepy feelings inside me. But the battle I have to fight now is with a tiny creature more deadly than a ward full of leopards.'

A screen was put round Yonah's bed. He was obviously seriously ill. After examining him I turned to Mwendwa.

'It is bad enough to have severe malaria but he has an infection of the brain as well.'

She nodded. 'That's what I thought, Bwana! Everything is ready for taking fluid from the spine.'

This was only a small operation but it would have been decidedly painful if Yonah hadn't been almost unconscious. We collected a test tube full of fluid from his spine. It looked milky. The microscope gave us the final answer. I came back to the ward.

'Mwendwa, it is meningitis all right. But thank God it is the variety that we have the answer for! Inject a million units of penicillin straight away.'

'Bwana, may I talk with you a little?' It was Baruti. 'Bwana, you have just said that we have the answer to this disease. Now, I think I have the answer to the leopard crisis. My plan is this…'

He sat down and talked fast and long. My eyes opened wider and wider.

When he stopped I said, 'This could cost you your life, Baruti. You realise that, don't you?'

'This I understand,' he replied seriously.

'And Yonah here, the one who better than any other could help you, can do absolutely nothing?'

Baruti nodded. 'I see that clearly but I have Jesus with me. He didn't hesitate when it came to dealing with sin and that does more damage than any leopard, or all the leopards put together. And Jesus said, "Greater love has no man than this, that a man lays down his life for his friends." Perhaps if I do this thing it will protect many people's lives and because of that some may understand what Jesus did on the cross.'

'But, Baruti, you don't think…'

He shook his head. 'Bwana, my mind is made up! I will do it tomorrow.'

14

Non-Poisonous

At dawn Baruti woke with a start. In his dream he had been pushing his way through a great spiky cactus trying to escape a charging rhino.

He smiled, '*Yoh-heeh*! It's a happy thing to wake from a bad dream and find that it was only a dream.'

Then he remembered. That day he faced an ordeal which would make his nightmare seem like a picnic. His mind flashed to the place where he had built the leopard trap, the trip-string which when touched would bring down the spike covered with poison - a spike so sharp that it would penetrate leopard's hide with ease, and poison so powerful that if enough of it was absorbed death would follow very quickly.

Through his mind flashed the pictures of the failure of all past efforts to shoot or trap that leopard, whose whole warped energy seemed to be bent on killing people.

He sat down and thought out his plans for the day.

First he sharpened his *panga*. The great knife might be needed to cut more thorns to strengthen the *ibululu*.

Into his bag he put the spike mounted in its block of hardwood, taking particular care with the poison-loaded black grease that covered it. He picked up the bag, locked his door and set out.

A boy he didn't know was squatting in the path near his house. Baruti greeted him cheerfully, '*Mbukwa*!'

'*Mbukwa*,' mumbled the lad and ran off downhill.

Baruti strode past the hospital and through the maize gardens to the church. Outside the door he put down his knife and his bag and went inside to pray.

The boy ran to a large tree where Juma sat waiting.

'*Amekwisha kweda kanisani*,' he panted.

Juma nodded and darted down a path well sheltered by standing corn. Working fast, he opened Baruti's bag, lifted out the spike, wiped it clean and smeared some similar black grease over the grooved nail.

He put everything back exactly as he had found it and slipped silently away.

Not far from his house stood Nungho and the boy. Juma nodded curtly.

Nungho sniggered, 'It was a good thought - he always goes there.'

Juma's lips parted in an ugly grin, 'That sharp piece of iron will anger leopard considerably and the medicine on it will give him pain but nothing else.' He put a shilling into the boy's hand.

Nungho protested, 'Great One...'

'Shut up!' snarled Juma, as he turned on his heel.

Baruti got up from his knees and went briskly down the path to the thornbush trap. He walked round it, cutting some more stout saplings and ramming them into place. At last he was satisfied that it would be a formidable barrier to any wild animal.

On the hill Tembo was standing on tiptoes to see what was happening.

'*Koh*!' he muttered. 'Why did I leave the telescope in the ward. *Kumbe*! The only way to see now is to climb...' He gripped the limb of a buyu tree and swung onto the branch above him. From there he had an excellent view of what was happening.

Against the boulders on the slope above the trap he saw a movement and then everything was quiet again.

Inside the trap Baruti stuck his *panga* in the ground and squatted down, chewing a piece of grass.

'*Yoh*!' he mused, 'I shall come here an hour before the time of sunset but without weapons. I shall come secretly as far as people are concerned. Nothing must keep the leopard away. He has deep cunning.'

He moved across to look again at the trap, adjusting the trip-string and fitting the poisoned spike.

Baruti thought, '*Yoh*! That should do the trick!' Sweat broke out on his forehead. 'If it doesn't...*koh*!... it can well be the end of me! But there will be a spear outside there in the shadow of that great tree. I'll drag that limb out of the escape corner of the trap and that will give me at least a chance!'

Then he thought that in the daylight things didn't seem to look half as dangerous or deadly as they did when the shadows were long. His mouth set into a grim line. He looked up at the sun. He still had eight hours.

From his vantage point up the tree Tembo shaded his eyes and gasped. Leopard was moving purposefully towards his friend. At the top of his voice he shouted a warning but the wind was blowing in his face. That shout damaged his throat and his voice became only a whisper. With horror he saw the leopard come closer and closer.

Baruti suddenly leapt to his feet and grabbed his *panga* as the great spotted cat stopped directly opposite him and snarled through the thornbush.

Tembo's mouth was dry. Through his mind shot the thought, 'Baruti is the bait in the trap! I must get help quickly!' His hands gripped the branch on which he had been sitting but his feet couldn't reach the limb below. He struggled. There was a crack. He hurtled through the air and landed flat on the ground. Darkness seemed to swirl round him. Dazed, he struggled to his feet. Fighting for breath he stumbled towards the hospital.

Baruti, holding the *panga* above his head, stood waiting as leopard crept into the entrance of the trap. He reached down and picked up a stout branch of thornbush. Leopard moved forward a pace, its cold eyes fixed on its prey.

Baruti thought, 'He has the ways of all cats. I must do my best to help him play the cat-and-mouse game. The more time this battle takes the better for me.

Everything depends on the poison having a chance to act.'

A purring snarl came from the great beast as a thorn tore at its ear. Strong jaws closed round the branch jerking it out of the way.

Baruti's eyes dilated as he saw a twig lodge directly below the spike moving it slightly out of place.

Leopard crept on and stopped with his whiskers almost touching the trip-string.

Baruti moved back a pace.

Leopard bared its teeth and slid forward.

Baruti stopped frozen to the spot.

Leopard had pushed the trip-string but the spike caught on the thorn twig. For long seconds nothing happened, and then the twig started bending with agonising slowness.

Leopard moved forward. The spike pushed into its flank but did not break the skin.

Baruti stood absolutely still while the leopard's baleful eyes glared at him, trying to mesmerise him.

Teeth bared, leopard moved forward again. Its head appeared clear of the thornbush passage, growling in triumph.

Like lightning Baruti rammed a branch of thornbush squarely into the snarling jaws. Leopard drew back and then in fury leapt at its adversary.

Baruti swung the jungle knife. It bit into the killer's head. Leopard shook the blood out of its eyes, which blazed with rage. Again it crept forward and crouched to spring. But the bleeding from the *panga* wound welled up and blocked its vision.

Realising this, Baruti lunged forward and struck again. The sharp blade sank into the animal's skull. It grunted and hurled itself at the hunter.

Baruti flung himself flat on the ground and saw the lithe body pass over him and crash into the thornbush fence.

Leopard's face twitched. The wild eyes lost their focus. A spasm ran through the great body. It clawed convulsively at the ground and rolled over - dead.

Down the hill rushed a group of men led by Mboga, waving an axe. Others held spears, knobbed sticks and knives. They tore at the thornbush barricade and tumbled into the *ibululu*.

Baruti sank down, sweat pouring from him. As they forced their way in he said, 'The killer is dead.'

They crowded round the great spotted animal cautiously. Daudi, a spear raised, went slowly across. With his foot he pushed up the yellow eyelid and touched the eyeball. There was no movement.

'*Yoh!*' he said, infinite relief in his voice, 'it is dead, truly.'

Mboga, close behind him, looked earnestly at the still twitching beast.

'*Yoh!*' he said, 'it is not as big as I had thought.' Then he grinned. '*Koh!* Have you noticed? It is amazing how fast the water in one's veins turns back to blood when the killer is dead!'

15
Spots for Sale

The African schoolteacher raised his hand. The members of the school band beat their drums and blew their fifes. A triumphal march was made up the hill, half-a-dozen stalwarts staggering under the weight of the great beast.

From all over the place people streamed up towards the hospital.

'The leopard is dead - the leopard is dead - the leopard is dead!' chanted the children. There was murmur among the schoolboys. 'It was a big one, the biggest I've ever seen!'

'*Yoh*!' said Tembo. 'Behold, I have never been so close to a leopard before!'

A chuckle went round the place. 'Somehow it is different when leopard is dead. *Heeh*! Look at those teeth - look at those claws! Fancy looking at that and it looking back at you! Fancy going into that trap with only a *panga*. *Yoh-heeh*! Behold, Baruti is a man of courage!' Mboga heard this and at the top of his voice called out, '*Yoh-heeh*! Do you notice that Juma has not come to share in the rejoicing with us?' His face was one vast smile. '*Koh*! But of course, it is easy to understand. It was the leopard who should have killed Baruti!' Then he shouted, 'Behold, I have a nice charm here - yellow and black it is. It will keep four-toed leopards from attacking anybody. I will let you have it cheap...'

Many people looked sheepish as they put their hands up round their necks to cover similar charms.

Baruti bent down and said to Tembo, 'Well, Small Elephant, what about fear now? The leopard who did so much harm is gone. Who could have fear of old Madole these days? But remember, taking the fear away is not the answer. In life there'll be other Madoles and more leopards.'

Tembo nodded and bit his lip.

Baruti started to sharpen his hunting knife and Daudi called out, 'Behold, he is going to skin the leopard.'

The people crowded round.

'If these claws,' Baruti paused, 'and these teeth had gone into my body I would be as this carcass is now.'

'And how would you feel?' said Daudi.

'*Kah*!' said Baruti. 'Now that is a different matter. It's a wonderful thing to know that even if death does come your way, all is well. That is where Jesus Christ comes in. He does not only help you in this life but when death comes he is with you and takes you to his

Father and he speaks for you to Almighty God. There is no fear in dying…you enter a wider country.'

Baruti picked up the spike.

'*Koh*!' said a schoolboy, 'I've seen that before - in the hands of Juma bin Ali.'

'Where?' demanded Mboga.

'Outside the church this morning early. Was I not sweeping out the classroom? Did I not see Juma hurry to the door, open a bag, take this thing in his hands, wipe off some black stuff and put other medicine on instead?'

'Black greasy stuff?' asked Baruti.

The schoolboy nodded.

'*Koh*!' exploded Baruti, 'no wonder the poison didn't work! That explains much.' He picked up the spike, gingerly ran his finger over the top of a little black grease that still remained and touched the tip of his tongue with it. '*Koh*! - *Eheh*!' he spat. 'It is the cactus juice that burns like fire! No wonder *Chewi* here was not poisoned!'

'There would be wisdom,' said Daudi, 'in seeing that hyaena of a Juma!'

'I will do that soon,' said Baruti grimly, 'but first I will finish the skinning.'

Quietly Nungho slipped through the crowd and away down the hill to the grove of baobab trees.

The skinning was quite a lengthy business done with extreme care. At last Baruti sat back.

'*Heeh*!' said Mboga, 'a beautiful skin, indeed. How much better for it to be there pegged out on a board than to be keeping the dew off an angry leopard.'

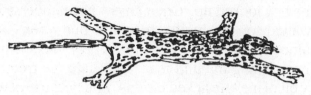

'*Eheh*!' said Baruti, but there was a grim look round his mouth. 'I am going now to deal with that hyaena Juma. *Koh*! Are not his ways those of murder?'

'*Eheh*!' said Daudi, 'he does not use a knife or a bullet or poison even, but with his cunning and his use of fear truly he is a murderer.'

'And to catch him,' said Mboga, with an impish look in his eye, 'you will need the legs of giraffe himself - for see, does not Juma follow the ways of hyaena and run at the time when it is safest?' He pointed with his chin to the dry riverbed. A yellow Landrover was skidding across it.

Baruti shrugged. 'There are some things you can't run away from.'

'*Eheh*!' said Mboga, 'those who have no joy in charms that don't work…'

'And those,' said Daudi, 'who have wireless sets and find out the secret of hiding stars behind moons.'

'Truly,' said Baruti, 'but these are smaller things. You cannot run away from God. You cannot hide from God. And there goes Juma, his back as firmly turned to God as it ever was.'

Tembo helped him carry the leopard skin back to his house to put it where hyenas could not get at it. Baruti sat back on his three-legged stool outside his house and smiled at Tembo who was drawing patterns in the dust with his finger.

The boy looked up. 'Great One, I have understood.' He waited for the hunter to speak but when Baruti remained silent Tembo went on, 'There was my great sickness killing me and fear that made me tremble - every bit of me.' He licked his lips. 'And because of what you told me and what you have done, I understand how Jesus can cure the sickness of the part of me that does not die, ever. And when I saw you in that trap - living bait - so that other people need not die, I understood better about Jesus and the cross.' Tembo drew in a deep breath and went on. 'Because I know that he is alive, fear becomes small.'

Baruti ran the back of his hand across his eyes and said softly, 'This is a thing of real joy, Small Elephant. This is the beginning. Keep travelling along this path doing what Jesus tells you in his book all the days that your soul is inside your skin.'

Tembo smiled. 'I have been thinking of the days when I become bigger. Mwendwa and Mali have taught me how to read. I shall go to the school here...' He started to push a pebble round with his toe. 'I have been watching the work of the hospital and they say that the days ahead will bring need for many to be doctors in this country. Perhaps I could become a doctor if I read very many books.'

Baruti looked out over the plains and nodded his head. 'It would be much hard work and much study but you could try. And, *kumbe*! Now that you have no one in your home to help and it costs many shillings to go to schools, is it not a good thing that you should have the skin of old *Chewi* here?'

He pointed with his chin to the wall of his house.

'These days, many shillings are paid for a skin such as that. This could start you on the way to doing this great thing.'

Tembo's face lighted up. 'But, Great One, those shillings could…'

Baruti interrupted him. 'It is a thing of wonder to turn a fear into a way of usefulness.'

16
Leg Work

That night there were festivities at the hospital. Drums were beating and people sang in a way that showed their vast sense of relief. The theme of song after song was 'The leopard is dead'.

Baruti was smiling. 'Things really have happened these days. Tembo has discovered the great secret. I only wish that Yonah Nhuti would find it too. I have searched right through my mind and I can think of no new way to help him to understand.'

'Did you not pray?' asked Mboga.

'I did pray and I asked God to show me a way.'

'*Kumbe*!' said Daudi. 'Sometimes he does things in a way different from our planning. Do you remember what happened to you in that leopard trap?'

'Can I ever forget?' said Baruti, 'It was uncomfortable while it lasted but God was there. God protects those who are in his family.'

'Truly,' agreed Daudi, 'but also, when his people offer for hard work he takes them at their word.'

Baruti laughed. 'I don't object to travelling uphill when I am doing it for him.'

There was a shouting and clapping of hands around the campfire and the drums beat with a rhythm that brought smiles to every face.

Rather anxiously Baruti looked across at me. 'If only they do not forget the great truth behind all these happenings!'

Mwendwa came towards us. 'Doctor, Yonah Nhuti is feeling a little better. He has a desire to talk.'

'Right, we will come.'

We went into the ward and sat down on each side of Yonah. His sickness had made his voice hoarse.

'*Hongo!*' he said. 'Tell me all that has happened. Here I have been lying with my wisdom on safari and my rifle asleep while much has been happening.'

'You speak wisdom, Yonah. Amazing things have happened. Baruti has shown the courage of a lion and by the skill of his hunting the four-toed leopard is no more.'

'Yoh!' said Yonah, putting out his hand, 'Baruti, you are indeed a man of strength!'

Baruti grinned. 'Do not forget that I used a stronger weapon than your rifle can ever be.'

'*Koh?*'

'*Eheh*! I prayed and I had with me One whose arm is stronger than that of any man, of any thousand men, of any million men; for it was Almighty God himself. *Yoh*! And he is strong!'

Yonah struggled up a little in the bed. 'Do you mean to say that God takes an interest in you and what you are doing?'

'*Eheh*! nodded Baruti. 'He does if you are one of his own sons…but you have to become a son of God.'

Yonah passed his hands over his eyes. '*Koh*! My head aches…'

'*Eheh*! We will talk more in the morning.'

Mwendwa came along with her syringe. 'Roll over,' she ordered, 'and be stabbed.'

A droll look came over Yonah's face. '*Yoh*! There is small joy in…*ooh*! *Eeh*!' The needle went in. He tried to grin. '*Koh*! To be hunted in a bed with a small spear is not a way of courage! The poor beast that is attacked, *kumbe*! - he has no chance.'

'Truly,' smiled Mwendwa, rubbing the spot where the needle had come out, 'he has no chance indeed, nor have the little *dudus* within him that produce the trouble. Think of the misery that is coming to them this minute as that medicine runs through your body. Now sleep, and sleep with skill.'

Outside they were still singing their songs of rejoicing.

Baruti gripped my hand. '*Kwaheri* - goodnight, Bwana!'

'*Kwaheri*, Baruti - travel under the shadow of his hand.'

Baruti looked up at the stars. '*Eheh*, Bwana, I will do that. I am doing his work and behold, perhaps the work I have asked him to give me will be rough.'

I did a round of the hospital.

All was quiet when an hour later Daudi strolled with me towards my house. We talked of this and that. Then Daudi said, 'In my bones I feel that things are going to happen.'

'*Heeh*! Things have been happening fast enough, thick enough, dangerously enough for months and months.'

Daudi grinned. 'Nevertheless, my bones - you know how my bones…'

'I know your bones, but…'

Through the night above the singing came clear-cut the *chenga* - the danger signal of the tribe.

We turned and hurried back to the hospital. 'I will run and find out what it is,' Daudi said, 'you wait at the office.'

A few minutes later he was back. '*Hodi*?'

'Come in. Trouble?'

'Slightly only for us, Bwana. It is Baruti - he has broken his leg.'

'Broken his leg?'

'*Eheh*! He was walking towards his house. He tripped, he fell and his leg is broken. There are those who would have picked him up and carried him in but he said, "No, I will stay here until the Bwana comes. I refuse to be moved."'

'He's right, you know. Is it a simple fracture?'

'Yes, Bwana - here.' He touched the bone between the knee and ankle. 'It is bent, Bwana, in a way that brings no joy.'

'Baruti knew that if he were carried the bone would

162

perhaps come through the skin and would cause real trouble.'

I picked up an emergency kit. Daudi had already brought splinting material. We hurried down the path. The crowd of people separated as we came up. Baruti lay with his head resting against Mboga. Young Tembo was standing back with a look of deep concern on his face. Quickly I injected medicine that would control even the most severe pain. Baruti's teeth were set and obviously he was in agony.

'*Yoh*!' came a voice. 'Why does not the doctor mend his leg instead of letting him lie there in great pain?'

Daudi replied quickly, 'It would make the pain worse to touch his leg until the medicine we've given controls the pain and then the doctor will help with greater usefulness.'

'*Hongo*!' said a voice. 'But is there medicine strong enough to stop pain of that sort?'

'*Eheh*!' said Daudi. 'And that medicine is already working within him.'

'*Heeh*!' came a sigh from Baruti. 'That's wonderful. *Kah*! That medicine - *heeh*! Does it stop pain!'

Those that stood around nodded their heads. As I set to work to deal with the broken leg, Baruti said, 'Bwana, wait a minute. All of you who look, you have no doubts that my leg is broken?'

'No,' came their reply. 'We have no doubt that normal legs do not bend in the odd way yours does!'

'*Heeh*!' said Baruti, 'and I too have no doubt that my leg is broken. Anyone who said otherwise would be a fool.'

'Truly, Great One, he would be a fool!'

'Now, your eyes tell you this thing as also do my eyes. But behold, the whole of my body screams to me that there is deep trouble and my leg itself is useless and I can do nothing to help myself. By having strong thoughts I cannot straighten my leg. By having money in my pocket I cannot take away the pain, nor do charms round my neck or medicine rubbed into my chest help. To fix this matter there must be someone who knows how to do it, someone who comes from outside.'

'Isn't that exactly what Jesus came to do?' said Daudi.

Carefully I pulled on the broken leg. Baruti clenched his teeth but fortunately as the leg was set there was no great pain. I put on a splint.

'The necessary thing is to straighten the crooked places.'

Down from the hospital came men carrying a stretcher.

'Baruti, we shall put you into the bed next to Yonah.'

'*Hongo*!' smiled Mboga, rolling his eyes. '*Yoh*! My words may sound mixed but I feel that your broken leg may be the key that brings light into Yonah's mind!'

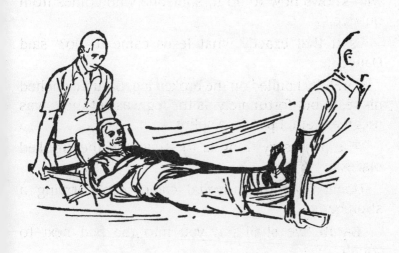

SAMPLE CHAPTER FROM:
JUNGLE DOCTOR
On the Hop

1
Invitation to the Feast

'Bwana, doctor, they're delicious roasted!'

Five heads nodded.

'Will you come and eat with us, Bwana?'

'Truly, Great One, it's a *sikuku* of great merit.'

Another voice chimed in. 'There is no meat as sweet to the palate as that of Panya.'

Out of the corner of my mouth I asked my African assistant. 'As the meat of what, Daudi?'

'Panya, the rat, Bwana,' he murmured, barely moving his mouth but rolling his eyes understandingly.

Louder he said, 'In the days of initiation into the tribe there is no greater delicacy than the roasted flesh of Panya.'

I turned to the boys. 'This is an invitation of great kindness but I would not rob you of your feast.'

A chorus of answers came:

'*Ng'o*, Bwana, there is plenty for all.'

'We caught a great heap of them.'

'There are eighty-seven, Bwana.'

'It would bring joy to your stomach.'

'Truly, they're delicious roasted.'

It was hard to keep a straight face.

'*Yoh*, behold it's a thing of sadness to me that the flesh of Panya, the rat, brings little joy to my stomach. Rather than reduce the size of your feast, let me add to it with another bringer of happiness.'

'*Sukari guru*,' came a voice, and they trooped off as Daudi picked up a saw and, in the room where we made medicines, cut a great block of brown, sticky, crude sugar into hunks the size of a closed fist. He picked up one of these, turned it over and prised out a cockroach which he flicked contemptuously aside.

'Eighty-seven rats is good hunting, Bwana. There is no shortness of food. Are you sure you will not come?'

I was sure.

At that moment, south of my ribs, I felt a fear growing that all was not well in the plains of Tanzania. Apparently I showed it for Daudi raised his eyebrows. 'Bwana, you feel that way too? It is well that Simba, the hunter, is with us.'

'*Eheh*, there is danger in the air – or at least something that smells like it. There must be thousands of rats about.'

'Truly, but that is because of the rainy season and the growth of the corn. There is food all over the place.

168

As he spoke a hawk swooped down on the peanut garden and was in the air again in a second, clutching a rat in its talons.

That evening the ominous voice was still loud within me. There were some clues that needed careful sifting. I took a book from the shelf, started to read the latest medical information on tropical disease and made page after page of notes. From outside came some loud yelling and from the cornstalk hut where Simba's initiation boys were camped echoed shouts of delight. Daudi came to the door to give me the night report of the hospital.

'*Zo'sweru*, Daudi – good evening, Bwana.'

'*Zo wusweru gwe gwe* – good evening to you, Bwana.'

'What's all the excitement?'

'*Koh*, these are big days in the life of an African boy, Bwana, these days of initiation. Listen. Simba teaches them special things. They rub their bodies with white pipe clay and they have a deep feeling of considerable importance within them. Are they not leaving childhood and becoming members of the tribe?'

'They may have joy, Daudi, but I have a hollow feeling as though something ugly is about to happen. I don't know what it is, but I'm convinced that it's my responsibility to stop it. If this vague threat isn't traced and stamped out, there could be terrible trouble.'

Daudi nodded. 'I too have this feeling inside me and it gives me no joy.'

I agreed. 'Perhaps the biggest thing that Christians can share is talking with God.'

169

Again Daudi nodded. Together we knelt and told God about it, asking for his wisdom and for keen minds to cope with any situation that might arise.

As Daudi walked back to the hospital, I settled down to read a chapter from the Bible, but I did not absorb much of it. It was about the Philistines fighting with Israel, but it did not seem to have any bearing on the problem. Rather abruptly I closed the book and prepared to go to bed.

Simba and his charges were still sitting round the fire outside their hut. He had obviously been telling them a story, for little gusts of laughter came on the evening air, followed by quiet singing. He was not only teaching them the ways of the tribe, but introducing them to the ways of the kingdom of God.

As I tucked in the mosquito net there was nothing to be heard outside but the voices of crickets.

It was a hot, windless night. I tossed about, thinking of this and that and planning the next day's operations. At long last came drowsiness, brushed suddenly out of the way by the grunting of a lion.

Shouting came from Simba's cabin. '*Mbera, mbera, lete wuzeru* – Quickly, bring a light!'

A handful of grass was thrown on the embers of the fire. The blaze showed up a large tawny-maned lion between the camp and hospital. More grass was heaped on the fire and a hundred anxious eyes watched the great beast walk slowly back through a gap in the thornbush.

For the next hour his grunting and roaring could

be heard. For me sleep had disappeared. I lighted the lamp and tried to work out a chess problem, but a procession of African creatures kept moving through my thoughts. Strangely enough, none of them was a lion.

'*Hodi*?' came a voice at the door, speaking in Swahili. 'May I enter?'

'*Karibu*, Simba. Come in.'

The broad-shouldered hunter entered.

'We seem to have visitors tonight.'

'*Eheh*, Bwana. Make no mistake, he will return. Not tonight, but some other time. I have examined his footprints carefully. He is a lion that limps – an old one. He no longer hunts buck and wildebeest and zebra. He goes for less nimble game.'

'Like you and me.'

Simba grinned. 'And the children, Bwana. What are we going to do about it?'

'There is my old rifle.' I pointed to an ancient .22, a most inaccurate firearm. 'But that would not even bend his skin!'

'*Eheh*, and if you wound a lion his rage is great. Lions are shy in the daytime, but at night they have no fear.'

'Did you not kill a lion once with a spear?'

'Truly, Bwana, but it is the sort of thing that you have no desire to do twice. I have had thoughts.'

'Have you? So have I. Nothing but thoughts all night long.'

Simba grinned again. 'Is it that lions scare you?'

171

'They do, but that isn't what scares me most. There is something vague and threatening that I can feel but I don't understand yet.'

'Bwana, let us then first deal with the lion.'

'*Viswanu* – right. What are your ideas?'

'I have arrows. I can shoot and not miss.'

'*Yoh*, but if you do, or if you merely wound?'

'Bwana, I will not miss but probably I will only wound. This is where I want your help. The lion must die quickly or people will. What I need is a poisoned arrow, one tipped with poison of strength.'

'We have what you want in my special cupboard with the skull and crossbones on it. But surely this is more a task for a medicine man than for me?'

The hunter grinned. 'We want to kill with certainty and speed, Bwana.'

I unlocked the poison cupboard. From a blue bottle I poured some white powder and took a dozen small pills from a glass phial. I ground these into a fine powder and mixed the lot into a paste with lanoline. Simba went to the door and came back with his bow and three arrows. Carefully this deadly ointment was smeared over the barb of each arrow.

'Watch that stuff. It's a mixture of two powerful poisons, strychnine and cyanide. If any of your hunters were to get some of that into them it would be the end – and quickly.'

Simba nodded. 'I will guard those arrows with care. Listen, Bwana.'

From further out in the thornbush came the roar of a lion. '*Hongo*, the walls of his stomach kiss each other, and he has no joy.'

'You think he will not return tonight, but the hearts of many people will beat more quickly than usual because of tonight's happenings?'

'*Ngheeh*, Bwana, and many will place outside their houses the special medicine they think keeps lions from entering. Behold, it is a good night for witchdoctors and darkness and creatures that slink.' Simba spat. 'Can you not feel that tonight is a night of fear and danger?'

Jungle Doctor Series

Jungle Doctor and the Whirlwind
ISBN 978-1-84550-296-6

Jungle Doctor on the Hop
ISBN 978-1-84550-297-3

Jungle Doctor Spots a Leopard
ISBN 978-1-84550-301-7

Jungle Doctor's Crooked Dealings
ISBN 978-1-84550-299-7

Jungle Doctor's Enemies
ISBN 978-1-84550-300-0

Jungle Doctor in Slippery Places
ISBN 978-1-84550-298-0

Jungle Doctor's Africa
ISBN 978-1-84550-388-8

Jungle Doctor on Safari
ISBN 978-1-84550-391-8

Jungle Doctor Meets a Lion
ISBN 978-1-84550-392-5

Eyes on Jungle Doctor
ISBN 978-1-84550-393-2

Jungle Doctor Stings a Scorpion
ISBN 978-1-84550-390-1

Jungle Doctor Pulls a Leg
ISBN 978-1-84550-389-5